# Honeymoon

# Cruise

# Murder

Dawn Brookes

# Honeymoon

# Cruise

# Murder

A Rachel Prince Mystery

Dawn Brookes

Oakwood Publishing

Paperback Edition 2020
Kindle Edition 2020
Paperback ISBN: 978-1-913065-19-5
Copyright © DAWN BROOKES 2020
Cover Image: AdobeStockImagesnapa74
Cover Design: Janet Dado

To Sue & Ruth

# Table of Contents

# Chapter 1

"You may kiss the bride." Rachel's father, the Reverend Brendan Prince, winked at his daughter.

Carlos didn't wait to be invited again. Applause rang out as he leaned in and kissed her tenderly before gathering her up in his arms.

"We made it," he beamed.

"We did." Her heart was too full of joy to say anything profound at this moment. The months of uncertainty over the wedding had taken their toll on their relationship. Carlos had accused her of delaying because she was too frightened to marry him. Rachel had known he was right, but hadn't been going to admit it. She had suffered recurring nightmares over the heartbreak caused by her previous fiancé Robert and how he'd broken up with her, dumping her for another woman.

Carlos had never wanted a big ceremony. He wanted to marry her with the minimum of fuss, with or without any guests if needs be. Sometimes she wondered if he would have preferred to fly away to some remote island and get married. One thing was certain; he had grown tired of her dithering and procrastinating. He had been determined the wedding should go ahead with no further excuses from her.

They'd locked horns as Rachel remained equally determined to have the big white wedding she had always dreamed of and wouldn't budge on that point. She eventually got her way, and once her fiancé realised how important the church wedding in her home village officiated by her own father was to her, he was humble enough to be gracious in defeat and apologise for his impatience.

Now they were Mr and Mrs Jacobi-Prince. Rachel had been loath to give up her surname, and would keep her maiden name Prince for her job as a detective sergeant anyway. Carlos hadn't minded in the slightest on that issue.

It had been a busy six months since she'd taken up the job in Leicester. Getting used to working with a new team took time. Her new boss was a workaholic, but then so was Rachel. Her first investigation had involved the murder of a sex worker, and she realised soon after that her world had changed. No more posh flat in London.

Initially she had rented a flat above a shop until she got to know the area. Then she and Carlos had put down a deposit on a house in Oadby, a village on the outskirts of the city.

Rachel's father had been preparing for his daughter's wedding over the past few months. Rachel worried he was taking too much on himself, so determined was he that his daughter would have the perfect wedding, knowing that she wouldn't be staying around for too long after the service, as the cheerful couple would be joining a Mediterranean cruise.

A few weeks before the planned day, Rachel had agonised over the matter of marriage and wondered whether her uncertainty was a sign that she should stay single. She had mistakenly shared her brooding thoughts with her mother.

"Don't be so ridiculous, Rachel!" Susan Prince had snapped at the idea when her daughter had tried to put it into words. "You're just plain frightened, like I was when I married your father. Every bride-to-be has nerves."

Suitably chastised, Rachel had realised it had been – as her mother said – pre-wedding jitters. She loved Carlos and wanted to be with him more than anything else in the world. The recurring dream of being jilted at the altar hadn't become a reality, and they were now husband and wife. Carlos placed his hand on the small of her back and she felt secure for the first time in months.

Life had been unpredictable for everyone else, too, as they'd all feared she would be the one backing out at the last minute. No-one had doubted Carlos's commitment.

The beaming faces of friends and family as she walked back down the aisle towards the opened doors of the church filled her with joy. Her bridesmaids followed her, chief of whom was her best friend Sarah, then her step-niece and Carlos's three nieces. Her cousin was a pageboy. She hoped this happiness wouldn't cause her chest to explode.

Carlos's best friend – a man she felt she knew already because Carlos had spoken of him so often – had flown over from Australia a week before the wedding to be best man. He had given Carlos his beloved springer spaniel, Lady, who now helped him with his work as a private investigator. Only a small party of Carlos's close family had managed to get over from Italy, and his parents were flying back this afternoon.

Sophie, Carlos's sister, followed them out and hugged Rachel. "Thank you for marrying my brother. You have made him so happy." The small, ebullient dark-haired woman loved Carlos, and Rachel couldn't help but like her and her geeky husband.

Sarah had stayed with her own parents, who lived in the same village as Rachel's parents, for the past week. The *Coral Queen* where Sarah worked as a cruise ship nurse had been in dry docks in Scotland for six months for a refurb, which Rachel was looking forward to seeing. Sarah had taken a job in a critical care unit in a London hospital during that time, finishing the week before the wedding to prepare for rejoining the *Coral Queen*. It relieved Rachel that her friend was returning to cruise ship nursing for selfish reasons: she couldn't imagine going on a cruise without her being there.

However, Sarah had appeared changed and more distant than usual over the past week. They had found little time to talk recently, except when surrounded by others for one rehearsal a few days before the wedding. Rachel wondered what was ailing her friend, but hadn't broached the subject. One day she would ask, but now was not the time for either of them.

The next hour passed in a blur of photos. Rachel didn't enjoy being the centre of attention; once the wedding ceremony concluded, all she wanted to do was to head down to Southampton to start the honeymoon on her beloved cruise ship.

"Rachel, you're more beautiful than ever." She didn't recognise the man bringing her to an abrupt halt, although the handsome face and sky-blue eyes were familiar. Perhaps it was a friend of Carlos's.

"It's Keith. Sarah's cousin. Don't you remember? I've been visiting my parents, and as your father put out an open invitation to the whole parish, I didn't think you'd mind if I tagged along with Mum and Dad. I've brought a few friends with me, too."

Slightly irritated, she answered, "Of course, Keith. How are you? Sarah told me you were in the village." *Warned, more like*, but there was no need to repeat what Sarah had said.

"I'm good, thanks. Although my one regret is that of letting you get away, and now look – it's too late, you're married. You know, I haven't found another woman quite like you. It was a shame about us."

*There was never an 'us'* was on the tip of her tongue, but what was the point? Keith had never been able to take rejection, even as a teenager, which was the last time she had laid eyes on him. Looking around for help, she realised that Keith had somehow cornered her while Carlos was entertaining the bridesmaids and her mother a few metres away.

"So what is it you're doing now?" she asked politely, although Sarah had already told her.

"I own a chain of exclusive hairdressing salons in central London. My main one attracts some big names."

*Here we go,* thought Rachel. *Me, me, me!* Sarah's cousin hadn't changed in the slightest. Sarah had mentioned Keith owned *one* salon, but he'd always been prone to exaggeration.

"That must be interesting."

"It is. I get to meet all sorts and hear secrets, if you know what I mean. Keeping my ears open lets me know who to avoid. There are some dangerous people who mix with the rich and famous." Keith dropped the showmanship for a moment and his face turned serious. "I hear you're in the police force now. That's another reason I wanted to meet up with you today."

"Oh?" Now he had her attention.

"I think someone is…" He looked down at his hands.

"Someone is what?"

"Look, I don't think this is the time to discuss it, but I understand you're going on honeymoon on that ship Sarah works on."

Rachel's heart dropped to her stomach. "So?"

"We'll be able to talk then." He grinned. "I'm taking a few weeks' holiday with my friends over there." He pointed to a group helping themselves to canapés put on for the guests, then turned back to her and leered. "I'm sure you won't want to spend the whole of the voyage in your suite, no matter how handsome your new husband might be."

Rachel glared. "That will not happen. If you have anything to tell me, now's the time."

Keith flashed her an irritating smirk and turned towards his entourage again, leaving her glowering after him.

"Darling," Carlos appeared at her side as Keith shuffled away, "who was that man?"

Rachel snapped, "His name's Keith Bird, one of Sarah's cousins. Not a favourite cousin by any means; he's always been eccentric and so full of himself. His parents still live in the village and, as you know, Dad gave out an open invitation." She huffed out a breath of exasperation. "So I guess he thought he would turn up for free champagne. And he's brought some friends along." Rachel pointed to a group of three men and a woman with Keith, helping themselves to more drinks.

"I didn't think the invitation included the population's relatives, and especially not friends of relatives." Carlos frowned. "You were flushed when I arrived. What was he saying?"

"Nothing of importance. He was being smarmy. He used to have a crush on me when we were at school, but I never liked him. Neither did Sarah, if I'm honest."

Carlos leaned in and kissed her on the cheek. "I expect every boy in that school had a crush on you if they had any sense. Anyway, don't let him upset you. A few extra guests aren't that bad."

He drew her back to join the main group. Photographs were being staggered so she could rest her smile in between.

"It's such a shame the cruise medics couldn't make it today," Rachel sighed.

"I know, darling, but you'll see them tonight at the on-board reception."

Tears filled her eyes suddenly and she tried hard to blink them away. Carlos drew her into his arms.

"Rachel, I know how sad you are that Marjorie couldn't make it, but her doctor said she couldn't risk being out, not yet."

Rachel nodded. "I know. I just wish we could have waited, that's all."

It was her new husband's turn to sigh. "She insisted that your father and I should not allow that to happen."

"Sorry, I'm being emotional. I guess a bride's allowed a bit of emotion on her wedding day. I'll be all right in a moment."

He pulled her close and kissed her forehead. "You're not really wishing we had delayed, are you?" The sensuous look in his eye made her laugh.

"No. I wouldn't have wanted to delay any longer. You know that."

Carlos didn't look entirely convinced, but took it at face value.

"You won't regret it. I will be the best husband you could ever hope for."

"Of that, I have no doubt." She kissed him tenderly.

Rachel couldn't bring herself to tell Carlos that Keith would be on their cruise. She wondered what it was the irritating man had to say, but dismissed it as nothing. He was playing games with her, as the one who had turned him down, and she would not let him or anyone else ruin her honeymoon. *No way, Keith!* She could easily avoid him; after all, there would be three and a half thousand passengers on board.

Sarah grabbed her arm while Carlos was talking to an old friend. They were out of earshot of the crowd.

"I saw Keith cosying up to you, Rachel. Sorry, I was on my way to rescue you when the photographer called the bridesmaids for a photoshoot. Please tell me he hasn't said anything to ruin your day?" Sarah's frown told Rachel that she too was angry that her cousin had made good on his threat to turn up at the wedding.

"He's just informed me he'll be on the *Coral* for the next two weeks," Rachel groaned.

Sarah's face reddened and she bit her bottom lip, a warning sign she was worried or concentrating. "Well, he won't be making trouble for you. Don't you worry, I'll have strong words. I've just about had enough of him and his clan. They've been coming around over the past few days and driving Mum mad."

Sarah stormed off, a woman on a mission. Rachel wondered whether her friend was diverting the anger sizzling below the surface from whatever was troubling her and almost regretted mentioning Keith's plans. Keith had better watch out, because Sarah was a pressure cooker waiting to vent.

The excess of happiness Rachel had felt a short while ago was waning. An ominous sense of dread took its place.

\*\*\*

"Time to go, Rachel," her father called.

Rachel checked her watch and hurried back to the vicarage to change for the road. There would be a reception on board the *Coral Queen*, so she would change back into her beautiful wedding dress later. She folded and rehung the precious garment carefully. The village had one of the few remaining independent bridal shops, where she'd had her dress designed. People came from miles around as the shop was renowned for its service.

Rachel checked the white taffeta dress for marks. It had a sweetheart neckline accentuated with silver sparkles around the bust and pearl beading down to the waist. The waist itself had a plain band of taffeta with a slim sparkly silver belt. Falling away from the waistline, there was an overlay of tulle in a fine rose-coloured floral pattern.

The bridal shop had designed the dress with a full-length veil and train trailing about two feet in matching tulle. Rachel could reattach the veil with a simple hair grip later on. She had rejected sparkly headbands and crowns, opting for simple elegance rather than anything overly fussy.

Rachel folded the dress over her arm and went downstairs.

Brendan Prince had arranged for Carlos's Ford Capri to be parked at the front of the vicarage after the guests had decorated it with ribbons. Thankfully, Rachel had asked her father to deter them from going overboard with the car, as it was her husband's pride and joy. They had agreed to make an early exit and meet the *Coral Queen* in time for the honeymoon.

Her parents were waiting outside the vicarage, Susan Prince chatting to Sarah's parents.

"Thanks for everything, Dad. You excelled yourself." Rachel couldn't have wished for a better wedding. How many brides get to be married by their father? The only downside was that he couldn't walk her down the aisle, but that was a minor price to pay. Her brother, David, had taken his place.

"Have you got everything, darling?"

Rachel noticed her mother's watery eyes. "Yes, Mum. Thanks for taking care of me over the past week. I couldn't have done it without you."

"I'm so happy for you, Rachel, and you, Carlos." Her new husband bent down to kiss Susan Prince as he relieved Rachel of the wedding dress and placed it carefully on the back seat. Then he opened the passenger door to let her in.

"Where's Sarah? I haven't said goodbye."

"She left half an hour ago, told me to tell you she'll see us at the party tonight."

Rachel waved to the gathered crowd of guests as Carlos drove slowly out of her parents' driveway. The journey passed by in a haze of mixed emotions and memories she was trying to capture so she could bore future generations. Carlos chatted away happily while Rachel closed her eyes, recalling every moment of the ceremony. She giggled as she remembered her little niece stepping on her gown as she tried to walk down the steps to exit the church. There hadn't been a lot of time to spend with people afterwards, but she was pleased they had opted to marry from her parents' home rather than on board ship.

Carlos pulled into the cruise terminal and handed his keys to a parking attendant who would park the car in a long-stay car park. The ever-efficient crew removed the heavy luggage from the boot and Rachel grabbed her rucksack, glad she had changed into casual clothes for the journey down. Carlos handed over the wedding dress and a crewman packed it into a cover for such occasions.

"Don't worry, sir. I will take excellent care of it."

"Thank you." Carlos then took Rachel's hand and led her away from the terminal entrance. "Come with me. I have a surprise for you."

Following her new husband towards a drop-off point away from the constant stream of arriving cars, she screamed with delight when she saw the Bentley. The snow-white hair of her dear friend Lady Marjorie Snellthorpe was the first thing she noticed as the old lady stepped out of the car. Rachel ran over and leaned down to hug her.

"Marjorie! It's wonderful to see you. This is the best wedding present ever."

"You didn't think I'd miss seeing you off on this special occasion, did you? Congratulations, my dears."

Rachel stepped back and appraised her friend. "You look well."

"I am well. I try to tell my doctor that I have the constitution of ten of my age, but he won't listen. You know what these medical people are like. Give them a bit of power and they lord it over us."

Marjorie had recently had a severe bout of pneumonia that had them all worried, but apart from looking a little pale, her friend appeared as healthy as ever.

"Anyway," Marjorie continued, "that's enough about me. I have something for you. It's a surprise. I had to arrange it through Carlos, as the cruise line were being rather stuffy about everything, so unfortunately it's not a surprise to him."

Marjorie handed Rachel an envelope.

"What is it?"

"Open it and you'll find out."

Carlos winked at Marjorie while Rachel opened the envelope. "You've upgraded us! Marjorie, that's wonderful, but you shouldn't have."

"Pah! What else am I meant to do with my money? If that doctor cocoons me any further, I'll not be here long enough to spend it on anything."

Rachel beamed. "You'll be here for many years yet. Thank you, Marjorie. Although seeing you is the best wedding present. We'd have loved for you to join us, you know that."

"Don't be silly. This is your time. I'm sure your new husband will allow you to accompany an old lady on her next cruise, though."

"We've already discussed that. The answer's yes."

"As if I could stop you two," Carlos laughed.

"We need to leave, mam," Marjorie's long-time chauffeur, Johnson, cut in. "Remember you're not supposed to be out for long."

Marjorie kissed Rachel on the cheek. "Goodbye, Rachel. Take care of her, Carlos, or I'll be after you."

Rachel hugged her friend again. "I'll email you now we have the suite with all-inclusive internet and bore you to death with photos and call you when we hit land."

"I've already seen some gorgeous wedding photos. Your mother has been texting me all morning. I love the dress." Marjorie's bright blue eyes twinkled as she wound the window down after getting into the car. "If there's a murder on board, do annoy Chief Waverley for me, won't you?"

Rachel's jaw dropped open. Carlos led her back towards the terminal, but not before wagging his finger at the mischievous Lady Marjorie.

# Chapter 2

Sarah slammed doors and fought with coat hangers while unpacking, furious at her cousin overstepping the mark yet again. How dare he take advantage in this way? She'd had no inkling that when he'd asked where Rachel would be going on honeymoon, he was planning on spoiling the party. Now, he was not only stalking her best friend, but he was on her beloved *Coral Queen*. As if the last few months hadn't been bad enough without this. It's not as if she even liked him. They hadn't met in years. And why the sudden interest in Rachel after all this time?

A knock at the door brought her from her angry brooding.

"Bernard! Am I pleased to see you." The beaming face of her Filipino colleague lit up the room and lightened her mood considerably as they hugged.

"I couldn't wait to see you, so I sneaked away from stock checking. I hoped you would be on board already."

"Come in. I was just unpacking." It felt so good to be back among friends after the rotten few months she'd had. "I've put the kettle on. What would you like?"

"Here, I've brought my own." He handed her a Lapsang Souchong tea bag and gleefully followed her to throw open the balcony doors, taking in a deep breath. "I have missed this ship, although it was good to have some time with my family."

"Have you seen any of the others yet?"

"Gwen got here last night. We had a drink together – I boarded last night too. My flight got in from the Philippines yesterday afternoon, and I've slept on and off ever since. I glimpsed Brigitte a few hours ago before she went down to the passenger lounge to check people in. We all have to go down there at two. That's the other reason I'm here. All the passengers have to complete thorough health questionnaires before they board. The cruise line's been clamping down on infections recently; the new rules are strict."

"I read about it when head office sent the pre-boarding information. It's so good to see you, Bernard. You look drawn, though."

"I had to take up some work in casualty in Manila during the long break while she was in dry dock. Perhaps the hardest few months I've ever had. The population is growing too fast. I'd forgotten what a luxury it is to work here."

"Me too. I worked in intensive care. I bet the kids were pleased to have their dad home."

"They were. My wife says I spoil them, but when I'm away so often, I can't resist doing that, can I? I think we all did a bit of extra work to keep the debtors away. Gwen went home to work in Australia, and – hot off the press news – Graham joined her."

Sarah raised a quizzical eyebrow. The team had been wondering whether the chief medical officer and the chief nurse were becoming an item. Bernard was always the first to pick up on the latest gossip and fill her in, but she could also trust him to keep secrets when necessary.

She grinned. "So you think they're dating now, then?" As she handed him his tea, he took another deep breath of fresh air from the balcony before rejoining her and flopping down in a chair.

"I know so."

"That's great news. Let's hope it works out for Gwen after her previous experience."

"Yes, but that man was married. She should have known better."

"He told her his marriage was all but over, though, didn't he? Then announced he would not leave his wife."

"That's what all men say when they want a bit on the side. Anyway, Graham is a widower, so I sense another wedding coming on."

"You're a hopeless romantic, you know. Not everyone can be as happily married as you. Mind you, I'm sure that's because you're away so much. No woman could put up with you twenty-four-seven."

Bernard put his hand to his heart. "You hurt me. That's the sort of comment I expect from Brigitte." For a moment, Sarah thought she'd really offended him, but his shaking shoulders told another story as he burst out laughing.

Sarah put her tongue out at him. "Have you taken a look around the ship yet?"

The huge smile Sarah knew and loved broadened. "She's even more beautiful than ever, newly decorated throughout. There are a few extra facilities for passengers, and brilliant news for us: the crew pool's been replaced with a new one. No more blocked pumps and 'not in use' signs. They've added a Jacuzzi and extended our bar so that it can take more seats. I met a guy who works in the engine room last night and he told me they've also done up the rooms below the water line."

Sarah couldn't wait to check out the ship for herself. She and Bernard were lucky as officers to have balcony suites. Crew below the water line shared tiny rooms with up to three other people.

"I don't suppose they made them any bigger, though."

"No, but he said the refurb has made much better use of the space with fold-out beds rather than bunks. That means they can have friends in or play games."

"Oh, that's excellent news. Easier for us too when we get called to emergencies. Have you met the new baby doc?"

Alessandro Romano, the ship's junior doctor, had returned to Italy to get married and it had been difficult finding a replacement. She'd kept in touch with Alex via email and he appeared to be extremely happy.

Bernard frowned for the first time since entering her room.

"Yes and she's nooooo baby!"

"What do you mean by that?"

He gulped down the rest of the tea and jumped up from the chair. "That, my dear friend, you will find out for yourself when you meet her. I'd better go and finish that stock check. See you in the passenger lounge later." He slapped his head. "I can't believe I forgot to ask about the wedding. I bet Rachel looked drop-dead gorgeous."

"Of course she did. Do you want to know about the dress?"

He put his hands over his ears. "No dress details, please. Although my wife will want to know. Text me a photo of the bride and groom and I'll send it to her."

"You'll see the dress later anyway. I'll tell you about the wedding tonight. Remember, we're at the reception after evening surgery."

"As if I would forget. The new girl's on call."

She laughed. "Don't let Graham hear you calling a doctor 'the new girl'."

Bernard left, chuckling away to himself. He was renowned for his mischievous ways, which was what made him so companionable.

Sarah stared at the view from the window. It was a beautiful sunny day. When she walked on to the balcony, she could see buses and cars in the distance. There was plenty of activity port side as crew got to work unpacking fresh food, cargo and equipment.

Yes, it was good to be back.

If only Keith had been teasing Rachel about joining the cruise today, things would be even better. Either way, she would have to deal with him.

\*\*\*

Gwen was in her office when Sarah arrived at the medical centre on deck two. The room was familiar with its enormous desk, separate seating area, table and the smell of percolated coffee. The décor, though, was very different. Splashes of colour brightened up the walls and the floor had a new carpet. The previous one had seen better days.

She whistled.

"Sarah!" The Australian accent was stronger since Gwen's return home. "It's great to see you again." Gwen hugged her. The senior nurse was a good friend as well as her boss.

"This looks amazing. Bernard was telling me about some of the improvements since the upgrade, and if this is anything to go by, I can't wait to see the rest."

"You'll like what you find. Good to have you back, Sarah."

"It's good to be back. Where is everyone?"

"Graham's showing Doctor Sin around. Brigitte and Bernard have gone down to the passenger lounge. I thought I'd wait for you."

Sarah was happy. She had missed the team and the camaraderie they shared. They had been through some tough times together.

"I take it Dr Sin's first name compensates for the surname?"

The corners of Gwen's eyes creased. Suppressing a laugh, she straightened up.

"Her name's Brillo. Brillo Sin."

Sarah couldn't control herself. "Poor woman! What kind of parent calls their child Brillo Sin?"

"Well, the surname's common in China – apparently, she's mixed heritage. I don't know how they came up with the first name. Her name's not the issue, however. Our new doctor's not as relaxed as we're used to. She informed me in no uncertain terms that the nurses – including myself – should call her Dr Sin!"

*Oh no!* This was all Sarah needed: a doctor who was above herself.

"Don't worry, Gwen, I'm sure Bernard will lighten her up, although I don't know that I could call her Brillo without laughing. Perhaps her friends call her Brill?"

"It's her first day, so we'll let her settle in. Hopefully we can knock a few of the rough edges off her shoulders."

Gwen sounded doubtful. Sarah had been hoping for an easy return to cruise life. They had a great medical team and had only once had a difficult member to work with: a nurse on probation, so at least they hadn't had to bow to her as a senior officer. Apart from the fact she'd turned out to be a psychopath, they had put her in her place.

"I'd better join the others. We're all looking forward to Rachel's reception tonight."

"Me too. Damn! I forgot to ask, how was the wedding?"

"Wonderful... mostly." The frown returned to Sarah's face as she remembered she still had Keith to deal with.

"Oh dear. Did something go wrong?"

"No. Nothing like that. It's just a cousin of mine turned up and gate crashed along with his friends. He used to fancy Rachel when we were at school, and he told her he'd see her on the cruise. He and his mates are boarding today."

Sarah felt the anger returning, but didn't want to rant on her first day back. It sounded like they would have enough to deal with coping with Brillo Sin. At least the thought of calling a caustic doctor Brillo brought a smile to her face. She was still chuckling as they made their way off ship to the passenger lounge.

# Chapter 3

Rachel thought she'd better change back into her wedding dress now that the safety drills were over, but first she wanted to explore the suite. Carlos was overseeing preparations for the reception in the Jazz Bar, having hired the room for the evening. He'd insisted he wouldn't come to their suite until after the reception.

"I want to carry you across the threshold just like I promised."

She had grinned happily, not quite able to believe they were married at last. Now, thanks to Marjorie, they could honeymoon in the luxury suite she had become so familiar with on previous cruises. It was even more luxurious following the ship's refurbishment. The decor was similar, but freshly done. Replacement furniture and Queen-sized bed made it feel like a palace.

When she'd stayed in this room for the first time, it had been courtesy of Queen Cruises. Another time was at the insistence of Marjorie when she had accompanied her on a later cruise. She fired off a quick text to Marjorie, thanking her again for the upgrade and telling her how good the ship looked on its return from dry dock.

A knock at the door broke through her thoughts. She knew it would be Mario, the butler for this and the suite on the opposite side of the rear deck.

"Come in."

The door opened and a beaming Mario entered with a champagne bucket and two glasses. Sarah, who had changed into her officer whites, followed him.

"Congratulations, Miss – erm, Mrs Rachel," the El Salvadorian said. "I meant to put this in here before you arrived, but have tough family in other suite."

"Well you won't need to worry too much about us. Carlos can do the fetching and carrying."

"Oh no, madam. I won't allow that. I'm thrilled for you both and I will be here for whatever you need. Where is Mr Carlos?"

"He's downstairs, checking on things for the reception."

"Can I get you ladies anything to drink?"

"I don't think I dare," said Rachel. "I don't want to spill anything down the dress. I'm amazed I've kept it clean this far, and anyway, I'd better get a move on."

Mario left them to it. Sarah rushed over to hug her.

"Congratulations, again. Can I help?"

"Yes please. The buttons are beautiful, but I won't be able to reach behind to do them up."

"I thought Carlos would be here to help."

"So did I, but he wants to carry me over the threshold later and said it would be bad luck to come in before that. It sounded like a good idea at the time, but now, I realise, totally impractical. If you hadn't walked in, I was going to call you."

Rachel stripped down to her underwear and climbed into the dress. Sarah moved the train to one side and fastened the fiddly buttons.

"It's a good job you opted for a shorter train," she remarked.

"That was deliberate because Carlos insisted I wear the dress to the reception here," Rachel sighed.

"Quite right too. You might as well get a full day's use out of it. I have to say, Carlos looked stunning in his grey suit."

"I know. A few of the younger women couldn't take their eyes off him. He didn't know where to put himself. By the way, where was Jason? I thought he was coming to the wedding. Don't tell me Waverley made him come back early?"

"No. Not that. I didn't want to say anything earlier, but he had a car accident yesterday. Someone pulled into the middle lane of the M1 at fifty miles an hour without checking their mirror. Jason swerved to miss him and ended up crashing into the central reservation."

"Oh, Sarah, I'm so sorry! No wonder you looked—"

"Looked what?" Sarah snapped, still not her usual self.

"You seemed out of sorts today. Is he all right?"

"He'll live. He had to stay in hospital overnight last night because he got whiplash when a car behind racing down the outside lane had to do the same thing he did and smashed into the back of him. Thankfully it was early morning or there could have been a pileup."

"Does that mean he won't be joining us at all?"

"Oh, he's coming all right." Sarah scowled. "He discharged himself from hospital this morning and got a friend to drive him down to the port. He's in a neck collar. That's all I know."

"You sound angry."

"I'm angry with the world at the minute, Rachel, but we can talk about that some other time. This is your wedding day and I won't let anything spoil it."

Rachel spun round and locked on to Sarah's face. "Sarah, you're my best friend. You could ruin nothing as far as I'm concerned." She noticed a moistness in her friend's hazel-brown eyes.

"Ditto," Sarah said, smiling.

"I assume everyone escaped from the accident unharmed?"

"Unharmed, and oblivious as far as I know. The man who caused the accident was unaware of the chaos he left behind or how close he came to death, I assume. Either that or he didn't care. The woman who ran into Jason was shocked, but not hurt. She might have some bruising from the air bag, but Jason checked she was okay."

Rachel held her breath. She had attended many road traffic accidents as a newly qualified police officer where people were not so fortunate. Sometimes mangled bodies had to be pulled or cut from wrecks. She shuddered.

"At least no-one died. Now, on to happier topics. Time to go, I think. Will my makeup do?"

"Yes, it's as good as it was this morning. Sorry we'll all be in uniform tonight, but at least I'm not on call unless there's more than one emergency."

"Who drew the short straw?"

"The new baby doc."

"What's he or she like?"

"I haven't met her yet, but from the little I've heard, she won't be anywhere near as amicable as Alex was."

"He's a hard act to follow though. I bet you miss him. Did he get married?"

"He did, last month. Now he's back from honeymoon and working as a locum until he finds a new job."

"I'm pleased for him, but let's hope your new junior doctor turns out to be as nice as the rest of you."

"If not, we will task Bernard with taking her in hand."

Sarah's voice was flat. Rachel's concern for her friend was growing, not dissipating. Was her angst worsened by Jason's accident and his stubbornness at insisting he join the ship? Honeymoon or not, Rachel would find out what was behind the sullen moods of late. Carlos would understand.

There was already a buzz in the Jazz Bar when they arrived. The band was playing some light music to greet the guests, but everyone stopped speaking when Rachel entered and a corridor opened up in front of her, lined by smiling faces. It was a small party with old friends and extended family, mostly Carlos's, who were joining the ship to wish him well. Other than that, it was the medical team and the security team with a few other crew members Rachel had got to know during her previous cruises and investigations.

Carlos didn't seem to notice the room had gone quiet. He was talking to an elegantly dressed and rather beautiful Italian woman Rachel hadn't met before – she must be one of his extended family. Carlos's brother, Marco, nudged him to let him know she'd arrived. His gorgeous brown eyes shifted from the woman he had been talking to and fixed on Rachel, his face flushed.

*Has he been drinking already?*

"Rachel, my breathtaking bride. Come over here, I want to show you something." Without introducing her to the woman he had been talking to, he took her arm and led her over to the side of the room where piles of gifts were stashed.

"Wow! How are we going to pack this lot?" she exclaimed.

He laughed. "We'll work it out."

She nodded. "We must."

Rachel turned back into the room, and she and Carlos went to join the medical team. Brigitte, the French nurse, was the first to speak.

"Rachel, congratulations. You made it at last. I wish you every happiness." The nurse air-kissed her on both cheeks.

"I don't know how a woman can be more beautiful every time we meet. The dress is exquisite." The voice was that of Bernard. Rachel had a particular soft spot reserved for the small man, waiting his turn to congratulate her.

"Shut up, you. I hadn't finished. What would you know about dresses?" Brigitte gave him the glare that *she* reserved only for him.

Rachel laughed. "I see you two are as friendly as ever."

The team formed a group around her, and she chatted happily. Carlos disappeared from her side, probably to speak with family. Then the one person she hadn't wanted to see headed towards her: Keith Bird, accompanied by the same group who had been at her wedding earlier.

Sarah blocked their path, preventing them from moving any further. There followed a heated discussion, and Rachel noticed her friend summon the chief of security, Jack Waverley, who had also been heading in Rachel's direction.

Following a brief conversation, the group turned and left, but not before Keith had hissed something in Sarah's ear. Her friend looked angrier than Rachel had ever seen her. It caused a knot to form in Rachel's stomach.

"Rachel?"

She turned her head as Carlos appeared once again at her side.

"Sorry, did you say something?"

"I said it is time to eat. They set the tables at the far end. Are you okay?"

"I'm fine, just a bit tired. I think I must be hungry." She didn't want to tell him that Keith was on board. He would want to know why she hadn't told him earlier, but even though Keith had gate crashed their wedding, she'd had no idea he would try to do the same with their reception. He always was a chancer. She just hoped that was all he was up to.

The thing that concerned her more than anything was Sarah. She should have contacted her more often than she had over the past few months, but she had been so wrapped up in wedding plans and her own work that she had neglected her best friend. She hoped that whatever was troubling Sarah would pass.

The tables seated eight people at each and waiters brought dinner up from the restaurant galley. After five courses, Rachel was feeling better.

"I hadn't realised how hungry I was," she said to Carlos. "I haven't eaten since last night."

He took her hand. "Me neither. The boys arranged a champagne breakfast this morning, but I couldn't eat. I was terrified you wouldn't turn up."

She laughed. "Now that would have been funny, since my dad was marrying us."

Her new husband saw the funny side and joined in with her laughter. Then the head waiter clinked a glass to bring the room to quiet.

"Ladies and gentlemen, it's time to toast the bride and groom, and then we'll have some on-screen speeches."

Rachel looked at Carlos, confused, as the people stood and raised their glasses.

"To the bride and groom." They spoke in unison.

"I have some secrets up my sleeve," Carlos whispered with a smile.

Next, a large-screen television flickered into life and there followed well wishes from friends and colleagues all around the world. Afterwards came a poignant speech from Rachel's father that brought tears to her eyes. Then the head waiter switched the television off and the Groom gave his speech.

Rachel couldn't have been more pleased with how it was going. She was not such a traditionalist that she would not give her own speech, so the best man introduced her, and she rose to the occasion.

She and Carlos had discussed it a few months prior to the wedding, and he was as keen as she that they start married life on an equal footing. Even her father, who was a traditionalist, had given his approval.

"Times are changing, darling. We must change with them," he had said.

"My husband and I would like to thank you…"

\*\*\*

Rachel's speech ended to exuberant applause and the music started up again, louder than before. Guests made their way through to the primary room where space had been cleared for dancing. Carlos took her hand and held her close as they enjoyed their first dance as a married couple.

"Brilliant speech, Rachel."

"Thank you. Yours wasn't so bad either." They laughed. "I haven't said hello to many of your family yet. Sarah's gang distracted me."

"Sarah will love to know she's in a gang – I'll tell her. Where's Jason? I haven't seen him."

Rachel explained about the car accident, but told Carlos that Jason was on board.

"So don't worry, you can do your ex-military man-bonding thing."

The lines around Carlos's eyes creased and the dark irises sparkled, both things she loved about the man she was dancing with. Then she remembered.

"I don't think I've met the woman you were speaking to earlier. Is she family?"

A slight hesitation alerted her. "What woman in particular? I've spoken to so many today. You know how it is – you're a man-magnet, I'm a woman-magnet."

"Neither of those things is true, nor do they sound like a good basis for a happy marriage."

"And yet, that's exactly what we will have. A wonderful marriage. I promise."

"So who was she? The one who looked like she'd stepped off the cover of *Vogue*. I'm sure you can recall who I mean now."

The music stopped. "Oh, there's Leo." Carlos left her standing on the dance floor and headed off to greet his uncle as the next tune started up. Too stunned to follow, she was temporarily shaken. This wasn't like him at all.

*What's the matter with everyone today?*

"May I congratulate you on your wedding, and on a fine speech." Waverley's voice brought her back to the present.

"Thank you. I'm pleased you made it. Did you have a pleasant break?"

"We did. It was good to be back on land, but it's even better to be back on board. May I have the pleasure?" He took her hand and drew her into a casual embrace.

"What did you do with your time away?" she asked as they moved around the dance floor with ease. Waverley was a more adept dancer than she'd realised.

"Brenda and I went home. We walked and talked, and although I felt guilty not working, we enjoyed each other's company away from the hustle and bustle of ship's life. I expect it was rather different for you."

"It was, but let's keep that conversation for another day." Rachel didn't want to remember any of the cases of the past few months. Especially not the gruesome murder investigation that had concluded just a few weeks before her wedding.

"I understand. Who was that man Sarah asked me to turn away? He told me he was a friend of yours."

"He's not a friend. I haven't seen him in years." She didn't mention he was Sarah's cousin, and for the second time that day, an icy shiver ran down her spine.

What was Keith Bird up to?

# Chapter 4

"So much for the free booze you promised. Now what?" Duncan was the first to complain following their forced exit from Rachel's reception.

Keith was sullen. He'd already had a shock meeting earlier – he couldn't believe it had been his ex-girlfriend, Esther, who had interviewed him. If he'd known, he never would have gone for the job. Now Sarah had made him look a fool in front of his mates. If he could call any of them friends, that was.

"I don't know about you," he said, "but I'm going for a smoke. There's a Cigar Lounge on the next deck."

"That woman had no right speaking to you the way she did. You should report her," Max grumbled.

Keith frowned. "As you well know, having met her a few times over the past week, 'that woman' is my cousin."

"Still, she was rude. Anyway, I'll join you in the Cigar Lounge."

It was always Max who followed him. He was like a hound dog that never gave his master a minute's peace. Keith tolerated the fat man because Max invested vast sums of money in his business – but hopefully not for too much longer, if Keith had his way.

"If you like." He shrugged.

The others had a brief discussion, which didn't include Max. Jean put herself forward as self-appointed spokesperson.

"We'll see you in one of the bars on this deck after your smoke."

"Right. See you later."

Keith was angrier now than when they'd left the Jazz Bar. Now he was stuck with Max and regretting the decision to take a cruise, especially following his meeting with Esther. There was no way she would take him on; she'd just wanted to see the look of surprise on his face when he turned up to the interview. He would never have worked for her anyway.

He'd applied on a whim, a crazy idea. A rush of madness had enveloped him when he fired off the application form, feeling the need to get away. But that matter remained and was playing on his mind. He had to speak to Rachel – she was a detective, so maybe she could help.

Max's squeaky voice broke into his thoughts. "You seem like you've got a lot on your mind. You've hardly said a word."

Keith stopped and stared at Max, whose forehead and upper lip were beaded with sweat following the brief excursion towards the Cigar Lounge. It always amazed him how quiet the big man's voice was, as if he were apologising for his existence.

Keith's malicious streak turned his frown into a forced smile. "I have, Max, as I'm sure you know."

The older man looked every inch the pathetic moron that he was. Keith would usually be civil, knowing how valuable Max's investment was, but at this moment he didn't feel the inclination to be so.

"I... I don't know what you mean," stammered Max.

Keith walked on with the other man scurrying uncomfortably close at his side, trying to keep up. He could almost smell Max's foul breath.

"There's a lot to manage back at the salon. Our client list is growing, and these celebrities are so demanding." Had Keith got the job, he was going to hand over the management of the salon to Duncan for a while. He'd already got a manager in place for the second venture, a new salon in Kensington.

"Oh that. Yes, I'm sure there is. If there's anything I can do to help—?"

*Like stay away, you mean,* thought Keith.

"No. Nothing. You do enough funding the place." Keith hadn't told Max about his new solo venture and had no intention of doing so. "I wanted to speak to Rachel, that's all, and now that's been scuppered." He lit a cigar as soon as they entered the lounge.

"Who's Rachel?" Max asked as they sat at a table.

Keith sighed, snapping, "Doh! The one who got married, the reason for us going to Brodthorpe. I've known her for years."

"Surely it can wait!" Max gawped. "She's just got married."

"The timing of her wedding is not my problem. She chose the day, not me. I need to speak to her in her professional capacity, although I did once hold a torch for her. Shame she's married an Italian, and a Jewish one at that."

Max choked on his cigar as a waiter arrived.

"Drinks, gentlemen?"

"Straight vodka," said Keith.

"I'll have a beer, please. You choose," said Max, regaining his composure.

Keith knew of Max's Jewish heritage, but he didn't give a damn about offending him. Neither did he care who Rachel had married; she meant nothing to him, other than a dent in his pride. What he cared about was his need to speak to her in her capacity as DS Prince.

"Could I have a card, please?" asked the waiter.

Keith didn't budge and Max obliged with what was expected of him, handing his card over to pay for the drinks.

Max turned to face Keith after the waiter had left. "Sometimes I think you say things like that to shock. I don't believe you mean to sound as prejudiced as you do."

*So the mouse has found a voice. I must have hit that nerve hard.*

"It's still a free country and I can say what I like, but the point is, I need to speak to Rachel Prince, or whatever her name is now, and my cousin will not stop me. I'll—"

"What?" Max was tapping his fingers hard on the table, an annoying habit at the best of times, but worse when he was under stress – and he appeared to be so now.

The drinks arrived; Keith ignored the question. He would take care of Sarah, but he wasn't going to tell Max too much.

"And what is Rachel's job?"

"Police."

Max spluttered his beer, causing the people at the next table to turn around. Keith smiled vindictively.

"Are you all right?"

Max wiped his mouth with the back of his hand. "I drank too fast, that's all. Went down the wrong hole. What do you want with the police?"

"That I can't tell you." Keith swigged his vodka, leaning back in the chair, feeling smug. Then he saw a man he recognised on the other side of the bar. He shot up straight in his chair and stubbed the cigar out in the ashtray.

"I'll see you upstairs."

*Had he seen him? What was he doing on this cruise?* Feeling it was right to be afraid after all, when he'd been ready to dismiss his worries, Keith headed downstairs at pace. Every so often, he looked behind to check he wasn't being followed. By the time he found the others in the Martini Bar, he was breathless.

"What's the matter with you, lovey?" asked Luke. The skinny man appeared to be holding court as Keith arrived.

"Nothing."

"Have you been running?" asked Jean.

"You're out of condition if you ask me, lovey. Perhaps you need to visit the gym while on board."

"Leave him alone," cut in Duncan. "Can't a man take a little exercise without the Spanish Inquisition?"

Keith nodded at Duncan, grateful.

"We were just talking about the new salon," said Jean.

*Typical big-mouthed Jean.* That's all he needed – her giving away secrets to the competition. Luke was an old friend from business school, but since Keith had decided to move in on the other man's patch, he was now a competitor. Keith knew Luke would find out soon enough, but he'd wanted to soften the blow as Luke was one of the few friends he trusted.

"Yes. Just down the road from mine," said Luke pointedly.

"Hardly," said Duncan, jumping to his boss's defence as he always did. Again, Keith was grateful for Duncan's loyalty, but felt his interest wasn't entirely professional.

"I was going to discuss it with you over a beer."

"Sounds as if there's not much to discuss, lovey."

Luke's tone was edgy. Keith couldn't blame him. He stared angrily at Jean – a brilliant accountant who saved him a fortune in tax. But the flaw in her character was uncontrollable. One day her gossip would cost him too much. He had tried talking to her about her loose tongue, and she always promised the earth but never delivered. She just couldn't help herself; she thrived on gossip. It was a shame because he fantasised over taking her to bed, but knew it could never happen. She wouldn't be able to stop herself telling the world about it if he did.

Then there were the clients who came to the salon. He had to hide their secrets from her, because if she found out the stuff some of them were involved in, there would be inevitable consequences. If it had been Jean recording customer conversations rather than Max, he would have had less trouble believing it, but he'd never give her access to the program.

He decided there and then. She had to go.

Keith finally spoke. "Let's talk about it some other time. I fancy another drink and Max's buying." He smiled up at Max, who arrived just in time to hear the announcement. "You don't mind, do you, Max?"

The fat man slumped down in his chair. "Not at all."

Keith could almost feel sorry for the six-foot four-inch giant. Max just wanted people to like him. Keith didn't feel that need himself, but recognised it in others and could take full advantage when required.

*\*\**

Luke avoided Keith for most of the evening, apart from shooting him the odd 'This isn't finished' look. Keith wasn't too concerned. Yes, he liked Luke, and preferred him to the rest of the present company, but in a choice between friendship and business, he would choose business every time. Money and power were overarching ambitions, and he intended to have both in abundance. Women were third on the list.

He glanced over at Jean once more. Her leaf-green eyes sparkled from the champagne. The flaming red hair, cut in a short bob, made her look slightly less feminine than he liked, but the full lips more than made up for it.

The alcohol was making him relax. Perhaps he would enjoy her this fortnight and then sack her when they got back to England. He might as well amuse himself.

She gazed over at him with a seductive smile. Duncan tapped him on the shoulder.

"I think you've had a few too many, boss. Shall I escort you back to your room?"

Suddenly alert to the unwelcome attention, Keith realised that they had all let their hair down. Duncan was giving him the come-on as Luke glared at them both.

Keith laughed a deep, guttural laugh, then his voice filled with sarcasm and disgust.

"I'm going for a walk." He pulled himself out of his chair.

"Shall I—"

"Alone." Keith held his hand out, palm towards Duncan. He stomped to the upper decks and found the pool area. It was quiet, as most people had settled in for the night. He leaned unsteadily on the ship's safety rail and stared into the night.

A few smooching couples passed by. It annoyed him that Duncan had broken through his fantasy; Keith was sure Jean wanted him to make a pass at her. He was also sure she had ulterior motives, but then so did he. Looking out into the black sky, he determined to pay her a visit before the night was out.

He heard laughter coming from his left and turned to see some of the wedding party enjoying late-night strolls. Sarah appeared with a chap in whites. Keith thought he looked Chinese.

"Just the person I need to speak to," he slurred.

Sarah halted. "You've got a nerve. As if you have anything more to say to me."

The man with Sarah stopped too.

"Lose the Chink," Keith snarled.

Sarah's mouth opened wide. "How dare you!"

"It won't take long. I just need to talk."

"Bernard, please excuse this ignorant goon. He's drunk. I'll see you in the morning, if you don't mind?"

"Are you sure?" the man asked.

"Yes. Thanks, Bernard."

"Okay. Goodnight. And—" the smaller man raised himself up until his face was within inches of Keith's "—I'm Filipino. Not *Chink*."

"Sensitive," Keith chuckled sarcastically as the other man left.

Sarah glowered. "I don't think you have anything to say to me, and if you go anywhere near Rachel, I'm warning you—"

"Is that supposed to scare me?"

But something in his cousin's eyes made Keith stop. He knew he had gone too far.

# Chapter 5

As soon as Sarah walked into the medical centre the next morning, she sensed something was wrong. Gwen was in her office, whispering to Graham. They stopped speaking when she walked in.

"Hello, Sarah. We were just talking about you." Gwen smiled, a look of sympathy in her eyes. "Coffee?"

"Yes please. Is that why my ears were burning?" Her eyes darted from one to the other. Graham gestured for her to take a seat in an armchair in Gwen's office. Something *really* wasn't right.

Gwen handed her a mug of percolated coffee, and then she took a seat in the armchair next to Sarah. Graham cleared his throat.

"I, erm… we have some unpleasant news, I'm afraid."

Sarah's head shot up from looking at her coffee. "Is it my mum?" Her mother hadn't been feeling well for a few weeks. Perhaps it was more serious than Mary Bradshaw had let on.

Graham shook his head as Bernard arrived and sat on the arm of Sarah's chair.

"I've just heard. How are you, Sarah?"

"Will someone tell me what's going on?" She noticed Gwen giving a quick shake of the head to Bernard, who took her hand.

"I'm sorry to be the bearer of bad news, but security found a man dead in the swimming pool in the early hours. This man was your cousin, I believe."

"Keith?" Sarah let out a vast sigh of relief. "Thank goodness."

Graham's mouth dropped open as he brushed back his greying hair with his hand. "Yes. A man called Keith Bird. Are we mistaken in thinking he was a relative?"

"No, you're not mistaken. I'm sorry, I didn't mean to sound callous, but I thought perhaps something had happened to someone close. I'm sorry to hear about Keith's death, but we didn't get on. What happened to him?"

"I'm afraid he may have fallen in and banged his head. The body... erm, your cousin's body was returned to England by the coastguard for post-mortem."

The realisation dawned on Sarah that the man she had been arguing with was now dead. How awful to yell at someone just before they died. She regretted being so sharp.

"I saw him last night. He was drunk, so it wouldn't surprise me if fell in the pool. To be honest, we argued. I was cross with him about something, not to mention he insulted Bernard."

"Oh?" Graham's eyebrows rose.

Bernard laughed. "Nothing I haven't heard before. He called me a Chink."

Graham frowned. "Hmm. Well, no wonder you were angry, Sarah. I would have been too. We don't tolerate racism on board the *Coral Queen*. I'm sorry that your last words were angry though."

"Me too." Sarah dropped her head, staring at her hands, recalling how she had shouted at Keith. "Good job it's not murder or I might be a suspect." Her laugh was forced as she realised what she had just said.

Bernard squeezed her hand tighter. Gwen took her other hand.

"You couldn't have known he would die. I'm sorry for his death, but I can't say I'm sorry that it hasn't upset you too much."

Sarah withdrew her hands, grabbing her coffee and gulping it down, hoping that she hadn't just incriminated herself if her cousin's death did turn out to be suspicious.

"Who dealt with the incident?"

"I did," a sharp voice snapped from behind. All eyes turned to look at a woman wearing drab, frumpy clothes who Sarah assumed was Brillo Sin. A mass of wild auburn hair fell shoulder-length around a rather plump face. The tight lips froze in what Sarah assumed was a permanent sneer and the nose stuck upwards, giving the impression there was an unpleasant smell in the room.

Sarah realised that she was gawping. Graham gathered himself together and broke the silence, smiling good naturedly.

"Sarah, this is Brillo, our new baby doc."

"Dr Sin," the woman corrected. Graham's steely gaze met her blazing eyes – eyes that matched the hair. There was little sign of the Chinese heritage that Gwen had mentioned in either her manner or looks.

*Perhaps her grandfather's Chinese*, thought Sarah, *and the influence had become too diluted by the time it reached Brillo.*

"We don't use formality when patients aren't present. It's first-name terms, Brillo." Graham's determined look challenged the doctor to argue with him. Sarah suspected that Gwen had already had words about Dr Brillo Sin with him.

"Good to meet you," said Sarah, opting not to use either name.

"Humph. Is there any coffee?" Brillo ignored Sarah and addressed Gwen, marching towards a chair.

*That's not how to endear yourself to the senior nurse*, thought Sarah. She sensed Bernard stifling a giggle.

"It's over there. Help yourself." Gwen nodded her head in the coffee's direction. The doctor opened her mouth as if to protest, but closed it again and marched towards the machine.

"Poor Brillo had quite an induction into medicine on the ocean waves last night. Thankfully, Brigitte was there to help. I was called shortly afterwards," Graham said.

"That Nurse Corbin was not much help. She didn't even know where the emergency bag was," Brillo sneered.

Sarah disliked the new doctor's open criticism of Brigitte, her friend and colleague.

"That's because she wasn't on call. I was," Bernard leapt to his colleague's defence. "And I believe we gave you an emergency bag to carry, Brillo."

Bernard glared at the doctor. He and Brigitte often disagreed and argued between themselves, but he would not let this newcomer stir up trouble.

"Yes, well," Graham intervened, "I'm sure Brillo will get used to how we operate." He turned to the new doctor, who had finally deigned to pour her own coffee. "Surgery starts in ten minutes. Why don't you bring your coffee through to my room and I'll fill you in on what's expected?"

Brillo shrugged in annoyance, but followed Graham. This woman wasn't going to be easy to work with. Brigitte arrived just as Brillo was leaving. The two women scowled at each other and Brillo barged past the French nurse – their clash the night before clearly wasn't over. And Brigitte was no pushover, as the new firebrand would find out soon enough.

"Close the door behind you, Brigitte," Gwen instructed. "I'll pour you a coffee."

Brigitte was clearly bursting to say something, as she kept opening and closing her mouth, shaking her head and pouting. The team didn't gossip, so she seemed caught in two minds. Gwen ensured they worked well together, and the petty squabbles between Bernard and Brigitte were harmless, so she let them sort those out for themselves.

They sat quietly drinking coffee, not mentioning the elephant in the room. Consumed by remorse over the previous evening's argument with her now deceased cousin, Sarah had other things on her mind anyway.

"I'd better start surgery," she said after staring into space for what seemed longer than a few minutes.

"Are you sure you're all right?" asked Gwen. "I can cover for you if you need some time to yourself."

"No, I'll—" Changing her mind, she said, "Actually, Gwen, I'd appreciate it. I *could* do with some time to myself. I'll return the favour if there's anything I can do for you."

"No need. I rarely get to do surgeries these days. I'll enjoy it."

"Who's on call?" asked Bernard.

"I am," said Brigitte.

"In that case, I'll cover it. Sorry you got called last night. Guest services mixed up the rotas."

Brigitte grinned for the first time since joining them, her sapphire-blue eyes flashing.

"Thanks, Bernard. I'm a bit tired. Sorry for snapping at you last night. I didn't realise you hadn't been paged and that new doctor did nothing but bark at me."

"Brillo's her name," said Gwen.

"Isn't that a scouring pad?" Brigitte grinned again. "Sounds about right to me."

"Okay, time to get to work, people," Gwen intervened. "You go get some rest, Sarah. I'm relying on you guys to be professional and help our new doctor settle in. If there's any atmosphere, it won't be coming from us. Do you understand?"

"I suppose," said Brigitte, sighing.

"We'll bring her around," suggested Bernard. "One of my stingers should do the trick."

"Don't you dare," laughed Gwen. Bernard's unique cocktail was renowned for its strength and had a love-or-hate reputation.

Sarah felt guilty taking time off when she'd only just returned to cruise ship life, but the incident with Keith was playing on her mind. Why had he wanted to see Rachel? She couldn't get how nasty she'd been to him out of her head. It was so unlike her, as if the volcano that had been bubbling under the surface from the stress of the past few months had erupted and poured red-hot lava all over her poor cousin. Not that Keith hadn't deserved a telling off; he had always been selfish, but gate crashing her best friend's wedding, then trying to do the same with the reception, was low even for him.

The weather was balmy and the sea relatively calm considering they were crossing the Bay of Biscay, so she went for a walk around the Lido Deck. She needed to talk to Rachel, but didn't want to bother her on her honeymoon. After all, that's what she'd been so angry with Keith about.

# Chapter 6

Rachel emerged from the bathroom into the large double bedroom that was separate from the lounge of the luxury suite. She had never felt so happy. Carlos had been everything she'd expected him to be during their first night as a married couple. They'd spent as much of the night talking as they had making love, and both were special to her.

She heard him speaking to someone in the lounge. Mario, probably. She pulled on the bathrobe provided by Queen Cruises and opened the door happily.

Carlos was on the phone. He didn't hear her and was speaking in Italian to someone, and he didn't sound happy. Shocked, she stepped back into the bedroom. As she did so, she heard him say, "*No. Non succederà. Non capisci? Era già finita da tempo.*"

She understood the sentence roughly meant, 'No. That's not going to happen. Don't you get it? It was over a long time ago.'

She made her second entrance more obvious. Opening the door, she called out, "Good morning, darling."

Carlos snapped into the phone, "*Devo andare* (I have to go)." Then he spun around and beamed at her. "And good morning to you. You were sleeping, so I let you rest." He crossed the room and kissed her full on the lips.

"Who were you talking to?" she asked after he'd finished kissing her.

"No-one."

Rachel's heart raced, fear threatening to overwhelm her. Carlos had never lied to her as far as she was aware. Why start now? They had only just got married. An icy dread came over her; she shivered, but decided not to challenge him. She didn't want to come across as a nagging wife so early in their marriage.

"I'll get dressed. Did you order breakfast?"

"Not yet. I was waiting for you to wake. What would you like?"

"To be honest, I'm not hungry. Shall we go for a walk?"

"If that's what you want to do." He kissed her again. "I love you so much, Rachel. Please know that."

"I love you too. I think I could get used to this marriage stuff. Thank you for last night."

He blushed. "We were wonderful together. I'm going to make you so happy, *tesoro*."

The Italian word for darling sounded so romantic coming from his mouth, she temporarily forgot the anxiety she had felt moments ago.

"I'll be back in a minute."

When Rachel returned to the bedroom to dress, she heard Carlos speaking again, returning the call. She felt a sudden wave of nausea overcome her and raced into the bathroom.

*This can't be happening.*

\*\*\*

An hour later, they were strolling arm in arm around the Lido Deck. Carlos appeared happy and was as attentive as ever, but the slight furrowing of his left eyebrow was a sign things were not perfect. He was worried about something, and what was worse, he was keeping it from her.

A ring of clouds filled the distant horizon, similar to the ones that had settled over her heart. This was not what she'd expected on the first day of her honeymoon. She breathed in the fresh sea air and decided Carlos had until tonight to tell her what was going on. After that, she would ask. A day that had started with so much promise was turning sour.

At least it couldn't get any worse.

"There's Sarah." Rachel saw her friend standing at the portside railing, staring out to sea.

"I thought she was working this morning," said Carlos.

They approached stealthily and Rachel cupped her hands around Sarah's eyes.

"Guess who?"

Sarah spun around. As Rachel released her, she noticed her friend had tears in her eyes.

"Whatever's the matter? Where's Jason?"

"Working. It's not that, it's—" Sarah's eyes overflowed and she turned away. Rachel put her arm around her.

"What is it?" Carlos asked gently.

Rachel noticed Sarah's bottom lip trembling as she bit it, a sure sign something was troubling her friend.

"Why don't we head somewhere quiet and talk?" she said.

"No, I'll be all right. I don't want to disturb your honeymoon."

Rachel took Sarah's shoulders and held her at arm's length.

"Tell me."

"I'll get us some tea," Carlos suggested. "Lady Marjorie swears by it."

Sarah gave a tearful chuckle. "Okay, yes please."

"We'll go up to the next deck." The noise from the pools was getting louder and the children splashing in the kids' pool were drowning out Sarah's voice. "The band is about to start up."

"I'll find you," said Carlos. "You two go."

Rachel took Sarah's arm in hers and they walked quietly towards the open steps leading up to the next deck. It took a few minutes to find an uninhabited spot where they could talk, but Rachel eventually saw a couple leaving a pair of sun loungers.

"There." She pointed.

The loungers were standing alone as the couple had likely moved them for their own privacy. Rachel and Sarah each settled on the edge of one and faced each other, Sarah biting her lip mercilessly.

"Come on, Sarah. What's the matter?"

"I don't know where to start."

"The beginning would be good."

Sarah took a deep breath and looked at Rachel through tear-filled eyes.

"You remember my cousin, Keith."

"How could I forget? I saw you having him expelled when he tried to gate crash our reception last night. What's he done now?"

"He... he's dead."

Rachel stared in disbelief.

Sarah continued, "He was found dead in the pool on the Lido Deck. Where we were just now."

"I'm so sorry, Sarah. I know you weren't close, but he was still your cousin. What happened?"

"It seems he slipped and fell in. The thing is, we argued."

"I know. That must be hard."

"Not at your reception. I met him later on the Lido Deck. He insulted Bernard and we argued. I was so angry. I can't remember ever feeling that angry."

Rachel's heartbeat quickened, "What are you saying, Sarah?"

Sarah bit her lip again. "I'm saying that I lost it with him. I yelled at him, even threatened him."

Rachel took her distraught friend's hand. "But you didn't—"

Sarah's head shot up. "Of course not! I didn't mean any of it. I just feel so bad that he bore the brunt of my anger over something else."

Rachel nodded. "Okay." She waited for her friend to continue. *Where the heck is Carlos?*

"It wouldn't have been so bad last night, but first he insulted Bernard, and then he said he would find you."

With a nagging doubt filling her gut, Rachel said, "He told me at the wedding he wanted to talk to me about something in my professional capacity. I dismissed it once he told me he'd be on the same cruise. I assumed he was up to his old tricks. When we were at school, he once said he'd found an injured cat, and when I went with him to check it out, he tried to kiss me. Needless to say, there was no cat."

Sarah's eyes widened. "You never told me."

"He was your cousin; I didn't want to cause you to fall out. Anyway, I kicked him in the shins, so he got his comeuppance."

Sarah smiled for the first time since Rachel had joined her, then frowned.

"You don't think there could be anything odd about his death?"

The thought hadn't escaped Rachel. "I hope not. Was he drunk when you met him last night?"

"Very."

"Well that makes it more likely he had a disastrous accident. I'm sorry, though. I didn't like him, but I wouldn't wish him harm."

*And I would have liked to know if he really had something important to discuss.* Rachel wanted to keep that thought to herself, but Sarah didn't give her the chance.

"I wonder if he wanted to talk to you about something serious. Although he probably was up to no good. I do feel better now, Rachel. I'm sorry to bother you when you're on honeymoon. Did you enjoy the wedding and everything?"

"Every minute. Did you know Marjorie met us at Southampton and upgraded us?"

"Yes. Carlos asked me to keep it secret."

"And I thoroughly enjoyed the reception."

"And afterwards?" Sarah laughed and Rachel smirked.

"Oh, that was by far the best part."

"I'm pleased. Anyway, I've taken up enough of your time. It seems Carlos has got lost. Perhaps he's still dreaming of last night."

They laughed again, but Rachel had an uncomfortable knot in the pit of her stomach.

"Do you want to join us for lunch?"

"No way! You go find your beau. I'll grab something to eat and then collect the on-call bag from Bernard."

"I thought he told me he was on last night?"

"Yep. There was a mix-up and Brigitte got called to attend to the drowning. So he's taken her on call this morning. The new doc upset Brigitte."

"Oh dear! Troubles in the medical team already? It's a shame Alex left, I liked him."

Sarah sighed. "Me too. This new one will be trouble. She's full of herself and seems to think nurses are skivvies."

"We can't have that. I'm sure Brigitte and Gwen will put her in her place."

"She tried to order Gwen to pour her coffee this morning, can you believe?"

"What did Gwen say to that?"

"More or less told her to get it herself, but in a polite way. Graham took Brillo – that's her name, Brillo Sin – out of our way soon afterwards."

Rachel laughed. "Poor Dr Bentley. He won't like disharmony in his happy team."

"He hates it. So does Gwen. Anyway, that's enough talk about Brillo Sin for one morning." Sarah checked her watch. "It's lunchtime. You really had better go and find your husband – I enjoy saying that. I'll catch you sometime. Enjoy the rest of your day. I'm so happy for you, Rachel."

"Thanks," said Rachel. Watching her friend go, she stood up slowly. It had been over an hour since Carlos had gone to get tea. Either he was giving her space to speak with Sarah, or...

The knot tightened.

# Chapter 7

Rachel went in search of Carlos, wondering whether Keith Bird really had been wanting to speak to her about something to do with her work. If so, it didn't bode well for his death being an accidental drowning. As a result, she worried about Sarah's argument with the dead man, especially the part about her threatening him.

*Let's hope there's nothing odd about the death.*

It could well have been accidental, from what Sarah had told her about Keith's drunken state. He was foolhardy enough to jump in the pool and bang his head, or fall asleep in the water. She had attended to a few cases of young men being dragged out of the Thames when she worked in London and, more recently, a young woman had been found in the River Trent after a drunken night out.

Rachel stood at the inner balustrade overlooking the Lido Deck, mulling over what Sarah had told her. The pools were full of people swimming or sunbathing around the sides. No-one would imagine that just hours before, a man had drowned there. The pool would have been drained, disinfected and refilled before being opened to passengers this morning, of that she was certain.

The figure of a familiar woman caught her eye. Rachel strained to see who it was through the glare of the sun; the earlier cloud cover was no longer on the horizon, and the sun reflected off the pool in full glow. The nagging feeling in the pit of her stomach returned as she recognised the woman and, more alarmingly, the man with her. It was undoubtedly the same attractive woman Carlos had been speaking to when Rachel had arrived at the wedding reception the previous evening, and now her husband of twenty-four hours was again in earnest conversation with this woman at the poolside bar. Was she who he had been speaking to on the telephone this morning?

Time stood still. Rachel found herself glued to the spot, captivated by the sight of her husband's attention taken up by this mystery woman's conversation, so much so he had left Rachel alone with Sarah. Anger, disappointment and an overwhelming fear threatened to engulf her as she stood motionless, holding on to the rail for support. The realisation that she could have married a liar dawned, taking her imagination to places she didn't want it to go.

The woman's olive skin glowed; her black hair, cascading down her back, shone in the sun. Her long legs, tucked elegantly under the table, revealed just enough flesh to annoy Rachel. A white summer dress hugged her thighs. She was stunning.

Now she'd had the opportunity to study her new rival, Rachel couldn't help thinking that last night may not have been the first time she'd seen her.

*Where have I seen you before?*

"Miss Prince… sorry, Rachel. How are you today?"

Waverley's voice yanked her from her dark thoughts. The familiar frame of the security chief, his thinning hair, as well-groomed as ever, and the pristine white uniform felt comforting at that moment.

"Good morning, Chief. I'm fine, thank you. I hear you've had a busy night."

Waverley coughed – never a good sign, as it usually meant he needed to say something delicate.

"It's only just afternoon. How on earth could you know about our unfortunate passenger? But I expect Sarah told you. I'm concerned about her. She doesn't seem herself."

As if realising he shouldn't be burdening Rachel with his doubts, he coughed again.

"Erm, where's your husband?"

"I'm right here, Chief." Carlos appeared, bright and breezy, on her right-hand side, carrying a tray of tea.

Waverley grinned. "Congratulations again to you both. I'll leave you to your married bliss. Good day."

After watching Waverley stroll away, Rachel could barely bring her eyes to meet those of her husband lest she betray what was going through her mind.

"Where were you? Sarah left ages ago."

"Sorry, darling, I couldn't find you. I think the tea's gone cold. Shall we get lunch?"

He was speaking too fast, plus the lack of eye contact confirmed what she already knew: he wasn't being honest. The last time he'd been like this was during her first cruise, when they had only just met.

"Did you meet anyone while you were searching?"

"It's hard not to run into people on a cruise ship. To be honest, I thought I'd let you have some time with Sarah. She seemed upset and maybe needed your help. What was it all about anyway?"

At least that part could be true. "You remember her cousin, Keith, who was at the wedding yesterday?"

Carlos's brow furrowed. "How could I forget a man who gate crashes our wedding and annoys my wife?"

"What I didn't tell you, because I'd hoped it wasn't true, was that he was holidaying on the same cruise as us. Yesterday, at the wedding, he said he wanted to talk to me in my professional capacity. I just thought he was winding me up. Sarah was livid."

"So she should be. She's discovered he's on board then. Don't you worry, I'll deal with him."

"Erm, yes, he is on board. Or rather, he was. He tried to gate crash our reception last night. You didn't see him because Sarah and Waverley dealt with him and his party of friends."

Carlos's jaw sharpened as he scowled. "First he gate crashes our wedding, and then he has the audacity to turn up at our reception. It's a good thing you didn't tell me, or *I* would have dealt with him last night. Some people have a nerve. If he comes near you again, you tell me." Suddenly he stopped speaking and a raise of the eyebrows replaced his scowl. "What do you mean, he *was* on board? Have they thrown him off?"

She glanced around to check no-one was listening to their conversation before lowering her voice.

"They found him dead in the pool in the early hours. His body's gone back to Southampton for post-mortem."

Carlos blew out a heavy breath. "That's all I need! Can't a man get married and come on honeymoon without all this nonsense?"

Her husband's petulance surprised her. "All what nonsense?"

Carlos seemed about to say something else when an uncle and aunt who had been at their reception the day before joined them.

"How is the lucky couple this morning? I take it you're not hungover, Carlos?"

"I'm not hungover at all, but then I drank nothing like as much as you, Leo." Carlos slapped the skinny man on his back. "Are you finding your way around the ship?"

"He's not long up." Leo's wife, Bella, rolled her eyes.

"Whereas my wife has been to the spa and found the shops. I must have a word with the captain about closing them." Leo's raucous laugh was infectious, and the other three joined in.

"Would you like to join us for lunch?" Carlos asked.

"Why not?"

"Leo, they are on honeymoon! Thank you for the kind offer, but we will join our table for lunch in the Coral Restaurant."

Suitably rebuked, Leo laughed. "It seems we must decline your kind invitation. Women always know best about these things. Some other time. You two enjoy yourselves. I remember what it was like to be on honeymoon." He winked at Rachel.

After the couple had left, Carlos took her hand. "He's right, women do know best. Come on, I'm hungry and you must be starving. You didn't have breakfast. Where would you like to eat?"

Rachel's appetite had disappeared, but she wasn't ready to tell Carlos that.

"I'll settle for sushi."

They headed towards the buffet. Being familiar with the routine, they used the hand disinfectant from the dispensers automatically. Then Rachel headed towards the sushi counter, while Carlos went in search of pasta.

They found a table for two, families and travel groups filling the larger tables as people came in from the poolside to eat. Some carried heavily laden trays back to the pool, others sat inside or in the overspill on to the outside. The buffet was always a free-for-all, but Rachel usually enjoyed the hustle and bustle. Today, though, her mind was elsewhere.

"Rachel, you've hardly said a word since we sat down." Carlos had almost finished his meal, while she had barely touched hers. "You are happy, aren't you?" His deep brown eyes held her gaze. If she hadn't witnessed him with the mystery woman, she would have fallen for the feigned hurt.

*You tell me*, she thought, but answered slowly, "I'm a little tired. All the wedding preparations and working up to the last minute must be catching up with me."

"Not to mention you didn't get much sleep last night." His upturned mouth revealed the dimples she loved.

"And that," she replied. "Carlos, what was it you were going to say before your uncle and aunt turned up?"

"I can't bring myself to call them uncle and aunt, especially as she's younger than I am." He laughed and tucked into the last remnants of his lunch.

"Well? What was it?"

"I can't remember. It was most likely something to do with Sarah's cousin being on our cruise. How's Sarah taken the news?"

"She's upset, but they weren't close. She feels guilty because they argued before he died. He apparently insulted Bernard, and she was furious. I believe there's more to it than that, though. She's not been herself for a few months."

"I bet Jason's accident has upset her, too, poor woman. Then her cousin turns up and starts causing trouble. I only hope there isn't any more to this death than a drunken accident, Rachel. Your reputation will be irredeemable if there's anything untoward." He smiled grimly.

"It was already, so that doesn't worry me. I am worried about Sarah, though." She felt it wise not to tell anyone, not even Carlos, that Sarah had threatened her cousin shortly before he died.

"Did anyone witness the accident?"

"Not as far as I understand. It doesn't seem likely— Sarah would have said if they had because there would be no doubt then. She feels guilty about the argument. She thinks she might have said things that were out of character."

Carlos whistled slowly. "From what I've seen and heard of this man, he would have deserved it. Are you saying she was most likely the last person to see him alive? If so, I hope for her sake it was an accident."

"I wonder what it was he wanted to tell me now. What if it was something that led to his death? I wish I'd paid more attention."

"Darling, you were a bride on her wedding day. Anyway, as you say, he's always held a torch for you. He was most likely mischief-making and trying to get you to pay him some attention. Some men are like that. If you ask me, there's too much mischief going on around here."

His sullen demeanour had returned.

"Carlos, I wish you'd tell me what's on your mind. I'm your wife now. We need to be honest with each other."

For a moment, he opened his mouth as if to deny anything was troubling him, but closed it again. He took her hand.

"I love you so much."

There was nothing else to say. He was not going to tell her about the woman she'd seen him with. Twice. Or was it three times?

She leaned back in her chair. A distant memory fluttered at the edge of her mind, and then was gone again, pushed aside by the stark truth. Her new husband wasn't being honest with her, and the realisation made her heart freeze over.

# Chapter 8

Evening surgery went smoothly, and Sarah felt happier about life. She had assuaged the guilt surrounding her last conversation with Keith, reasoning that she'd had every right to be angry about both his behaviour towards Bernard and his gate crashing her best friend's wedding and reception. As Keith had been her cousin, it was natural that she'd feel responsible for his actions, even if feeling so was irrational. He was an adult and therefore responsible for his own conduct. Talking to Rachel had helped, as it always did.

Bernard poked his head around the door. "Have you eaten, Sarah?"

"Not yet. I was busy this afternoon. There were several mishaps in the bars."

Bernard's eyebrows hit the ceiling. "You're telling me. I've had an evening surgery full of drunken accidents. I guess it will be one of those cruises. There are quite a few sizeable parties on board."

Sarah shrugged. "I met a member of one of them this afternoon. A twenty-five year nurses reunion party. Some of them were hilarious, but they had been enjoying numerous cocktails in the Cocktail Lounge while reminiscing about times gone by. One of them had twisted her ankle, but nothing too serious."

"Ooh, I look forward to meeting them. How many?"

"Around fifteen, I think. Not all of the training set could get away. You'll love them, lively and entertaining. I also saw security breaking up a fight on deck sixteen after a clash over people hogging sun loungers!"

"I'd have liked to see that. Anyway, Brigitte, Gwen and I are going to dinner. Seems none of us has had time to eat today. Are you coming?"

"What about the docs?" asked Sarah, secretly hoping Brillo Sin wouldn't be joining them.

"Graham's on call and doing room visits. You know how some passengers need the reassurance of meeting the chief medical officer. That other woman has gone for a lie down after her – I quote – 'Trying night working with a French nurse who doesn't know what she's doing.'"

"So much for Gwen saying she'll settle in soon."

"Perhaps she'll feel better after some sleep. It was a baptism of fire coming across a dead body on her first night. Let's forget her. Come on, I'm starving. The others have left already. I said we would meet them in the officers' dining room."

By the time Sarah and Bernard arrived, Gwen and Brigitte had found a table for four and Gwen waved for them to come over.

"Hello, Sarah. You look better than you did this morning."

"I feel better. It all seems surreal now, as if it never happened. I've decided not to feel guilty about arguing with my cousin. How was I to know he was about to die?"

"We might have known with Rachel Prince on board there would be a death. At least it wasn't a murder," laughed Bernard.

"I've told you before, don't joke about such things. Remember, I had to deal with that poor man." Brigitte was never one to appreciate Bernard's gutter humour, as she called it. "He was handsome, you know, so sad."

Sarah wasn't sure what Keith being handsome had to do with his untimely death being sad, but was in no mood to dwell on the topic of her cousin.

Gwen looked across at her. "Will you be all right for the on-call tonight? I can do it if you'd rather not."

"I wouldn't hear of it. You've already covered one surgery for me today. No, I'll be fine and hope for a quiet night. Sorry you had such an awful time, Brigitte."

"Made worse by a certain doctor," laughed Bernard.

"Bernard, that's enough!" said Gwen. "We just need to give... erm, Brillo time to settle down to our ways. We don't know what she's been through."

"A car wash, by the looks of her hair," said Bernard, causing them to burst into fits of giggles.

It was good to be back with friends. Sarah knew that together they could cope with anything, including their difficult new colleague. She scanned the menu and relaxed, conscious that all would be well again now she was on board the *Coral Queen*.

Following dinner and some friendly banter, Sarah's radio burst into life. She got up from the table and dragged the on-call bag towards her.

"See you later, guys." She paused and turned back to the table. "Thanks for everything. Things can only get better now for all of us."

"I'll drink to that," said Bernard, holding up his wine glass in salute as she left.

Sarah pressed the call button on her radio. "Hello?"

"There's a man on his way down to the medical centre. He's asthmatic and has breathing difficulties. Dr Bentley's busy with another passenger. Can you see to him?"

"Yes. I'll head down there now. What's his name?"

"Mr Andrew Farmer. His stateroom is 8665. A waiter is accompanying him to the medical centre."

"Thanks. On my way."

Sarah pulled the heavy trolley bag behind her as she made her way down in the service lift to deck two. Raggie, the medical centre steward, was still clearing up after evening surgery.

"I've got a passenger on the way down, Raggie. Is there a room ready?"

"Yes, Nurse Sarah. All the rooms have been cleaned and disinfected. Help yourself. Can I get you some coffee?"

"That would be great, thanks. I had dinner, but didn't get around to coffee."

"I'll call the kitchen now and let the patient in when he or she arrives."

"It's a Mr Farmer. A waiter's bringing him down. Let's hope he won't need a bed." The medical centre had a ward where they could admit passengers and crew when needed, and a recent addition was a high-dependency room with a mechanical ventilator. They had not yet used this, but she knew the day would come when it would be necessary.

Sarah opened up one of the consulting rooms and fired the computer into life, bringing up the details of Andrew Farmer.

"Mm, interesting. He's a government minister, fifty-one, history of asthma." It relieved her to see from his records he had never required ventilation or a hospital admission for the condition. Patients who had previous admissions by implication had a more severe form of asthma and were much harder to treat. Asthma could still kill people.

She heard the outer doors open and Raggie speaking to someone.

"Thanks, Gerome, I'll take it from here. This way, sir."

A small, dumpy man with a flattened face rather like a bulldog's entered, gasping for breath. He was sucking his lips in while trying to breathe.

"Good evening, sir, I'll be with you in a moment. Over there, Raggie, please." Sarah nodded to a chair next to an examination bed and, more importantly, the oxygen supply. Addressing the man's pleading dark green eyes, she nodded calmly.

"Mr Farmer, I'm going to give you some oxygen to help with the breathing and prepare a nebuliser. Have you ever had a nebuliser before?"

Andrew Farmer shook his head. Sarah realised that his fear was threatening to overwhelm him. Applying the oxygen mask over his face, she spoke calmly and firmly.

"The nebuliser is just a more concentrated way of giving you the salbutamol that you have in your inhaler. Don't be alarmed. Please try to slow your breathing down. The oxygen will help. Raggie will show you how while I get the nebuliser ready."

The medics had taught Raggie how to assist in emergencies like this and he was competent at it. Sarah didn't want to ask Andrew Farmer any questions at present, as the priority was to get the attack under control. Listening to Raggie calming the man down while checking his pulse and oxygen saturation via a finger monitor, she had the nebulised salbutamol going through the oxygen mask in minutes. The man visibly calmed as the solution reached his lungs.

Sarah sat with him for the first five minutes and watched his oxygen saturation improve, going from 90% up to 99%. The treatment was working. His blond hair was still soaked in sweat, but the colour returned to his face quickly.

She handed him a call bell. "I want to allow the nebuliser to do its thing for another ten minutes, so I'm popping next door. Call me if your breathing gets worse."

Sarah found Raggie wiping down the doors of the ward.

"Thanks, Raggie. He'll be fine. You don't have to stay. I'm sure you need to eat."

"No worries, I've eaten already. Your coffee is in Sister Gwen's office. I can listen out for our patient, if you like?"

Sarah grinned. Raggie had to be the most helpful attendant in the world and was an absolute rock as far as the medical team was concerned. He always knew what they needed, often without being asked, and his conscientiousness meant they never had to worry about checking up on him or his work.

"That's kind. I'll start the consultation on Gwen's computer. Call me when the nebuliser's through, and then you really should go. You've had a long day."

"Okay. Deal," he said, smiling brightly.

When she'd enjoyed her coffee, Raggie let Sarah know the nebuliser had finished. She returned to the consultation room to find Andrew Farmer a changed man: confident, chatty and in full control.

"Good to see you looking better," she said. "Do you mind if I ask you some questions now?"

Sarah took down his medical history and noted the time of the attack and what treatment he had taken before coming to the medical centre.

"This is a smart operation you have here. I never imagined there would be such facilities on board a cruise ship." He whistled. "Yep, a fine setup."

"Thank you, Mr Farmer. We do our best."

"Oh, none of that. Call me Andrew. Everyone does."

Sarah noticed him sucking in his lips again. Although he was friendly, there was something shifty about the way he stared at her computer screen.

"I take it you haven't cruised before, Mr... erm Andrew?"

"No. Can't think why. I like the luxury, if you know what I mean. I'd never thought of it before, but I heard a friend was coming on board and I thought, why not? Next thing, I asked my secretary to book this trip, and here I am. It's summer recess. I'm Minister for Housing, and believe me, after the year I've had, I need the rest. The PM's had a tough year, too, as you probably know."

"To be honest, I'm not really into politics, but I realise it's been a tense time in the UK. I spend most of my time at sea, and when I'm not, I catch up with family and friends."

"Lucky them," he leered.

"Does the friend you mentioned realise you're ill?"

"Oh no. In fact, he's not a friend, more of an acquaintance. He's my hairdresser, or should I stay stylist? Runs an upmarket salon in Knightsbridge. He doesn't know I'm on the cruise at all. It was a spur-of-the-moment thing—"

As Andrew nattered on, Sarah sensed the colour was draining from her face. Keith ran an upmarket salon in Knightsbridge. He had bragged to her parents about all the fancy clients he got in – she'd heard him mentioning various celebrities and politicians, most of whom she had never heard of so she had taken little notice.

She realised Andrew had stopped speaking. Looking at the expectant flat face, Sarah pulled herself together.

"I noted from your records that you smoke cigars, Andrew. In view of your asthma, it might be worth considering quitting."

"My, you medical people have one-track minds, don't you? I was asking where I could get myself a haircut while on board."

"Sorry, we tend to be that way. There's a salon on deck sixteen. You can make an appointment through guest services or call them from your room. The number will be in your information pack. Now, about the cigars—"

"Well, I appreciate the advice, Nurse, and I'll think about it. Thanks for the help tonight. How do I pay?"

"Our senior nurse does the billing. She will add it to your cruise statement. If you're using an insurance company, you can let us have the details and we'll contact them for you."

"Right, I'll drop off the details in the morning. Thanks again—" he stared at her name tag, "—Sarah."

Something about the way he said her name made her cringe.

"Say, does that thing give you information about all the passengers on board?" He'd stood up to leave, but turned back as if remembering something and nodded towards her computer. "I wouldn't mind saying hi to my hairdresser while on board – you never know, he might do me a favour and give me a trim. Could you look up a Keith Bird?"

Sarah held his gaze without flinching. "I'm sorry, Andrew. Guest information is strictly confidential. Perhaps you could phone him or leave a message at guest services."

"Of course, I should have realised that. Thanks again, Sarah."

Sarah stared at the door for some time after he'd left. Something about the apparently innocent questioning didn't sit right. What had he been fishing for, and why did she get the feeling he already knew about her cousin's death? At least he couldn't have known Keith was her cousin, but Keith's death was striking her as more significant than it had at first seemed.

She cleared away the nebuliser equipment, taking the machine through to the used area for Raggie to clean in the morning. After returning to the consultation room, she was placing her finger on the mouse to close the computer down when a thought struck her. She sat, pressed a tab and pulled up recent consultation history.

Her mouth dropped open as Keith's details came up on screen. The last consultation, entered by Gwen, recorded the time of the body's departure to Southampton and the name of the coroner the death had been referred to. She clicked another button to look up the time and date the record was last accessed. Today's date, 21.39. The same time Raggie had let her know the nebuliser had finished.

She stared at the screen, realising Farmer must have pressed the tab 'find patient' to access the record. There had been enough time for him to do the search, as the medical team could open two patients' details up at the same time for simplicity. All he'd had to do was close Keith's record down again with a click of the mouse.

*Blast! How could I have been so stupid?*

She heard footsteps coming back towards her room. Had Farmer left the outer door open when he'd departed?

Her heart raced as the door to her room opened.

# Chapter 9

Running around the track on deck sixteen the next morning produced the desired effect. It invigorated Rachel. There had been no further lapses on Carlos's part and no sign of the mystery woman. He had been attentive to her every need throughout yesterday and she'd decided not to quiz him about the woman, or even mention her again.

Carlos had always been the most trustworthy man she had ever met, certainly not given to clandestine meetings with beautiful women without purpose. She trusted him. As for the idea that she might have seen the woman before, she'd dismissed that. She was probably mistaking her for a famous model or actress.

The more she thought about it, the more convinced Rachel was that Carlos must be arranging a honeymoon surprise for her, which would explain why he didn't want to speak about it. With one earpiece in, she relaxed as she listened to her favourite singer, Ed Sheeran, while running circuits. Afterwards, she headed into the on-board gym for a workout.

"I've been waiting for you. I thought I'd find you here."

It surprised Rachel to find Sarah sitting in the reception.

"Don't tell me you're here for a workout? You look as though you've been up all night."

"That's because I have. I was on call and barely got to bed before the alarm went off again. I'm here because I wanted to catch you alone, otherwise poor Carlos will be thinking I'm going to ruin his honeymoon."

"Our honeymoon." Rachel laughed, but stopped on noticing Sarah wasn't joining in. "Is this about Keith?"

"Yep."

"Would you rather grab some breakfast? I've done enough exercise for today."

"What about Carlos?"

"He'll be fine. I left him fast asleep; he said he wanted to catch up with friends and family this morning anyway."

"On honeymoon?"

Rachel laughed again and took her friend's arm. "Sarah, we will never be a couple who lives in each other's pockets, you know that. I think he's arranging a surprise for me. I keep seeing him in secret meetings with a woman. At first I thought it was odd, but now I suspect he's organising something, so I'm leaving him to it."

"Do you know this woman?"

"No. That's why I thought it was strange. She's probably a member of your hospitality team."

Sarah's raised an eyebrow. "Oh, tell me she looks like the back of a bus and weighs eighteen stone."

Rachel grimaced. "More like an Italian version of a Greek goddess. Drop-dead gorgeous, to be honest. I had all kinds of doubts going through my mind; I was getting paranoid, but Carlos is Carlos. There has to be an innocent explanation, and a surprise is the only thing that makes sense."

"I agree with you. Carlos wouldn't be carrying on, so I'm sure you're right. We've taken on a raft of new people in the hospitality team, including a new cruise director. His assistant is being described as gorgeous by some of the guests – I can find out if that's who it is for you if you give me a description."

Feeling a little bad about going behind Carlos's back in this way, Rachel gave Sarah a description of the mystery woman. The two friends collected breakfast served at the buffet bar, Rachel opting for mixed fruit and strong coffee, while Sarah had a full fry up. Then they found a quiet table.

"Something odd happened last night, Rachel."

"Okay. Go on."

"I treated a man for an asthma attack down in the medical centre. A rather smarmy man, if I'm honest. Anyway, that aside, it turns out he's a government minister."

"Interesting, but not odd," said Rachel as Sarah filled her mouth with bacon. "They allow government ministers holidays, you know."

"The odd thing is that it turns out he was one of Keith's clients."

Rachel nodded. "Now that is more interesting. So Keith's boasting about meeting important politicians was true. Still, coincidences happen."

"Except that Andrew Farmer admitted he'd booked on the cruise after hearing Keith would be taking it. Not only that, but when I was out of the room, he accessed Keith's medical record, then asked me if I'd tell him what room he was in."

Rachel had a sinking feeling. Was it something underhand that had led to Keith Bird's death after all?

"Let me get this straight. Andrew Farmer, a government minister who says he knows... sorry, knew Keith, arrives in your consulting room last night and you believe he took a sneak peek at your cousin's record?"

"Yes. That's about the sum of it. Don't you think it's strange?"

"How would he even know how to do that?"

"I left the computer running because Raggie was with him while the nebuliser was going through. Our system's designed for simplicity once the program's open. He was on his own for minutes, but that's all it takes."

"Perhaps he did just want to find out which room Keith was staying in so he could get in touch." *Who are you trying to kid, Prince?* Rachel kept that thought to herself.

"Then why ask me for the same information?"

"I don't know. Maybe he felt guilty or didn't get time to see the room number before you got back. Or perhaps he saw that Keith had died and was shocked. He could have been asking you about him, hoping you'd tell him what happened."

Sarah stroked her chin and stopped biting her bottom lip. "I didn't think of that. It could have been any of those things. They all make sense. I guess I'm jumpy because of the argument, and I'm still wondering what Keith wanted to talk to you about. It's also—"

"What?"

Sarah giggled. "Well, you know, Rachel. It's because whenever you're on board, there's always a murder."

"Don't you start! I bet that's the first thing Bernard said when a body turned up."

"Erm... Yes, he did, as a matter of fact."

It was good to see Sarah laugh again.

"Joking aside, you've put my mind at rest. Thank goodness for that. If I hadn't been called out half the night, I would have been awake imagining all sorts of things. What little sleep I got was restless. By the time I woke up this morning, I thought Keith had been murdered."

A cough interrupted their conversation, and one look at Waverley's face told Rachel that Sarah might just be right.

"May I join you, ladies?"

Sarah gulped, but said nothing. The lines on her forehead deepened and her wide eyes fixed on Waverley, who also had a not-slept look about him.

"Please do," said Rachel. "We were just talking about Sarah's cousin."

"I heard." The second cough and frown were a dead giveaway. "I'm sorry to have to tell you this, Sarah, but your cousin's death wasn't an accident. The coroner called late last night. There was no fluid in the lungs and the bruising to the back of the head is consistent with a severe blow from a heavy implement. Following a search of the area around the pool, we discovered one of the fire extinguishers had been removed from its strapping. I've put it aside for forensic examination once we return home, but I believe it was used to hit your cousin."

Sarah paled, but remained silent.

"Do you have any suspects?" asked Rachel.

"We interviewed the friends he came on board with yesterday as a matter of routine in case any of them had seen him before he ended up in the pool or witnessed the accident, but might have been afraid to come forward."

"The accident that's now murder," said Sarah in a squeaky voice.

"The thing is, Sarah," Waverley continued, "they all confirmed that Keith Bird was blind drunk, but one of them," he looked down at his notepad, "a Miss Jean Sutton, said she saw him arguing with an officer in uniform." He coughed again. "The description fits with that of yourself. Did you argue with your cousin on the night of his murder?"

Rachel gasped. "Surely you can't think Sarah had anything to do with his death?"

"It's all right, Rachel, calm down." Sarah looked towards the security chief. "Yes, we argued. I've felt guilty about it ever since, but I can assure you I had nothing to do with his death. Until this point, I was convinced it was an accident."

Waverley's voice became taut. "But I overheard you say just now that you thought it was murder."

Rachel breathed out heavily, her muscles tensing as she stared with disbelief from Waverley to Sarah.

"Sarah witnessed something odd last night. That's what we were talking about. It seems there's a politician on board ship who may have known Keith Bird. Sarah believes he sneaked a look at her cousin's records while she was out of the room."

"I think you'd better tell me what happened." Waverley used his hand to indicate to a passing waiter that he would like a drink.

"Yes, sir?"

"Could you bring another pot of coffee and a mug for me, please?"

"Right away, sir."

Sarah relayed the events of the previous evening again while they each helped themselves to fresh coffee. Waverley listened, interrupting occasionally to ask for clarification.

"So he could be another suspect." Rachel glared at Waverley.

"Compose yourself, Rachel. I don't believe Sarah did this any more than you do, but I have a witness who says she heard them arguing and that Sarah threatened her cousin. Now all I have in terms of Andrew Farmer accessing the dead man's record is Sarah's word against that of a pillar of the community. Farmer could argue that Sarah accessed the record herself and is trying to frame him because he mentioned knowing Keith Bird. You can see how it looks."

The tension in Rachel's neck tightened. Waverley was right. This wasn't looking good for Sarah.

"What are you going to do?" she asked.

"I will investigate – that's what I do – and hope that I can track down the killer before the end of the cruise. At least the friends of Sarah's cousin have informed me they are staying on board to complete their holiday. If I'm honest, there was only one who appeared upset, and that was a stylist who worked for him. If you ask me, I think he was in a relationship with Keith Bird, or at least he implied it."

"No way!" Sarah exclaimed. "Keith was straight, of that I am certain. He left a trail of women behind him and fancied Rachel like mad. That's why I was so annoyed with him. I thought he was mischief-making and might ruin Rachel's honeymoon. That's also why I asked you to throw them out of the wedding reception."

"Can I have the names of his friends?" Rachel asked.

Waverley peered at his pad again. "Duncan Fairchild is the man who implied he was in a relationship with the dead man. The woman who witnessed Sarah and Mr Bird arguing is called Jean Sutton, and—" His eyes rose from his pad to Rachel's. "Hang on a minute, why do you want to know? Rachel, I forbid you to get involved in this investigation. Leave it alone. Besides, you're on honeymoon."

Rachel thrust her jaw forward. "While there is even a hint of Sarah being under suspicion or in any way implicated in this death, you can be assured, Chief, I will do everything I can to hunt down this killer and see whoever it is brought to justice."

Waverley blew out a heavy breath.

"Rachel, I think the chief's right," said Sarah. "You should stay out of it. I feel guilty enough about the argument and that my cousin was trying to ruin your honeymoon without it defaulting to me being the one who put the kibosh on your long-awaited holiday."

"Carlos wouldn't want it any other way. In fact, he'll insist on us helping." Rachel sounded more certain than she felt. Carlos had been patient waiting for their wedding day and so looking forward to their honeymoon that she couldn't be one hundred per cent sure.

"Does Jason know about this?" Sarah asked Waverley.

"Not yet. I've been trying to get him to rest up following his accident, but I'll have to tell him. I would try to tell him he's too close to the matter and not to investigate, but I know how that feels and he won't listen."

Rachel nodded, understanding. Waverley's wife had come under suspicion of murdering a man on a cruise to the Canaries, and Waverley had been told to stay out of it. He had been at his wits' end, and Jason had disobeyed orders to keep him informed of developments. Waverley owed Jason, and there was no way that Sarah's fiancé would keep himself in the background.

"I don't want him hurt. He should have stayed home after his accident. I'm putting you all in danger and wrecking things." Sarah stood up, bleary-eyed, and left the table. "I'd better get to morning surgery."

Rachel stared after her friend. "This is not what she needs."

Waverley stroked back his thinning hair. "I'll find whoever did this, Rachel. We will put every person in the security team on the case. It has to be one of the dead man's friends. I can't see it being the politician Sarah mentioned, but we will look into him."

"Are you going to tell me who the other friends are? I think I met some of them when Keith brought them to my wedding."

Waverley shrugged. "You'll find out anyway. Just keep me informed, that's all I ask. There are two other people in the group. Luke Connelly – Miss Sutton suggested he was annoyed with Mr Bird over something."

"Did she say what?"

"I don't seem to have written it down. It just sounded like tittle-tattle, and remember, at the time I thought it was an accidental drowning. I suspect Miss Sutton is a gossip; it was hard to shut her up, now I think of it."

"What was Jean Sutton doing at the time she says she saw Sarah arguing with Keith?"

"Ah, that I do remember. She said she was concerned that he had seemed very drunk – smashed, I think she said – and followed him to check he was all right. Witnessing the argument, she described him as giving as good as he got, so she left them to it and went to bed. The last person in the group is a Maxwell Holloway, Mr Bird's business partner stroke investor in the business."

"So that could be a motive," Rachel suggested.

"I don't think so. He's extremely wealthy and a silent partner in the business. Left the day-to-day running and management to Mr Bird, he told me. He's a nervous type considering he towers above me. He informed me that he's also funding the cruise for all of them at Keith Bird's request. Rather generous, if you ask me. And there is one other person who knew the dead man. She's a member of staff on board, and apparently an old flame."

"Oh? That might be the actual reason for him being on board the same ship as my honeymoon, rather than because of it."

"The strange thing is, he applied for a job on board as a senior stylist. Our salon manager Esther Jarvis – Keith's old flame – interviewed him. She was shocked to hear of his death and quite upset when I told her about it yesterday. I think there may have been some bad blood between them – again, according to Miss Sutton – but Esther denied that, said their breakup was mutual. I have no reason to disbelieve her. She isn't aware we are now treating the death as murder."

"Did she know it was an old flame she would be interviewing?"

"Not until boarding day. They select interviewees via head office. He must have applied through one of our recruiting agencies."

"Seems a bizarre thing to do. He was running a successful business with well-to-do clients like Sarah's politician – she said he's a government minister."

"Perhaps he needed a break. Who knows why people do the things they do? I've given up second-guessing people, but in this case it would help to know if he was running away from something."

"Or someone," added Rachel.

"Esther's been with us eight years – one of our success stories. She's worked her way up from the bottom. I don't believe she will be in any way connected to the man's death, but we'll interview everyone again today to see if their stories hold up now we have more details. We must check their alibis. Although, from the sounds of it, all Mr Bird's group were 'smashed', as Miss Sutton put it." Waverley got up with a sigh. "I'd better go and tell Goodridge that his fiancée is the prime suspect in a murder investigation. That's a conversation I'm not at all looking forward to having."

*Jean Sutton goes straight to the top of my list*, thought Rachel. She could have waited until Sarah left and then hit Keith Bird. Rachel was ready to believe Jean was the last person to see Keith alive rather than her best friend, but why? Jean needed to have an apparent motive, and that's what Rachel was going to find out. Passion or money – which was it?

# Chapter 10

By the time Rachel got back to her suite to take a shower, Carlos had left. A note on the coffee table told her where he'd be if she wanted to join him and his friends. He had placed a red rose on top of the note.

She twirled the rose between her fingers as she thought about what to do next. A glimmer of a doubt crossed her mind as to whether she should leave the murder investigation to the security team, but experience suggested that might not be such a good idea. Waverley often jumped to the wrong conclusions when it came to murder. She wished Marjorie was with her, so she'd have someone to discuss it with, but the major thing bothering her was whether it was right to keep it from Carlos. If she could guarantee he would help rather than suggest she left it to Waverley, she would tell him in an instant. She wanted to avoid any friction because his previous reactions to her investigating murders on board the *Coral Queen* hadn't been positive. He had been more patient than any man on earth could be waiting for her to marry him; she just couldn't bring herself to ruin his idyllic honeymoon.

Mario knocked on the door before entering the suite. "Sorry Miss… erm, Mrs Rachel, I thought you were out. I was going to clean the room. Is there anything I can get for you?"

"Would you mind bringing me a pot of coffee and leaving it on the balcony, Mario? I'm going to take a shower." She had another thought. "Oh, and Mario? My hair was beautifully arranged for the wedding and it seems to be losing its style. Do you know if someone senior in the salon could redo it for me?"

"I will phone and make an appointment for you. The stylists are most likely booked up, but I can have a word with the manager, Esther Jarvis, and explain. I'm sure she will fit you in if they cannot."

Just what she had hoped. "Thanks, Mario."

\*\*\*

Forty-five minutes later, Rachel entered the hairdressing salon on deck sixteen. She had never been here before; it was impressive. Stylists were busy at each mirror, with passengers spaced evenly around the room, and the familiar aromas of hair product permeated the air.

She approached the reception desk where a short, lean man lifted his head and smiled through over-white teeth.

"Can I help you, madam?"

"I have an appointment with Esther Jarvis. My name's Rachel Jacobi-Prince."

He looked at his computer screen. "Mm, I can't seem to find you on here and Ms Jarvis rarely does hair, but please, take a seat and I'll find her. She may have booked it herself and forgotten to tell me. Wouldn't be the first time." He pouted as he stood up and retreated to the back of the salon and into an office.

Rachel picked up a magazine and leafed through the first few pages. Before long, an attractive woman with long, wavy hair came towards her. Esther Jarvis was immaculately presented, and a professional makeup artist could have applied her makeup it was so well done. Tight-fitting clothes accentuated her hourglass figure.

She smiled at Rachel. "Mrs Jacobi-Prince, welcome to the Coral Salon and congratulations on your wedding. Mario asked me to restyle your hair. Is that right?"

The salon manager spoke in a clipped, efficient tone containing no warmth. Rachel wouldn't hold that against her, as it must be hard trying to be interested in people's hair all the time. She was more a fitness fanatic than a glamour puss herself, and Carlos often reminded her that she was lucky that her looks and naturally blonde hair meant she didn't have to make as much effort as some people.

"Yes, thank you for fitting me in. It's just that the style I came on board with seems to be falling away."

"It looks pretty good to me." Esther flicked back her hair as she spoke. Rachel knew her excuse for being in the salon was weak, but she hadn't expected her new hairstylist to rebuff her.

"It doesn't feel right." *No, it doesn't feel right*, Rachel thought, *talking about hair as if I care that a strand has moved out of place.* Nevertheless, she was here now, so she had to put on a magnificent act to convince Esther Jarvis to spend some time over it.

"Please, follow Pierre, he'll prepare you. Mario said you didn't need a wash?"

"That's right. I went for a run this morning, so showered afterwards."

Was that a tut Rachel heard?

"If you'd like to come this way, madam," said Pierre, pouting even more that he was being asked to do something that clearly wasn't within his usual remit. Pierre helped her on with a gown and invited her to sit at the back of the salon. "This is for platinum passengers usually," he whispered.

"Oh, how exciting!" she exclaimed, clapping her hands gleefully like a silly schoolgirl. *Don't overdo it, Rachel*, she told herself.

"Can I get you anything to drink, madam?" Pierre obviously believed he'd made an impression and got the response he had desired. He stopped pouting and showed the teeth again.

"Tea would be wonderful, if you have the time. I'm sure you're very busy."

Pierre's grin widened and he tapped her hand. "I'll make time for our newlywed. We haven't had a bride in here for a while."

Rachel had barely sat down when Esther appeared behind her, running her long fingers through Rachel's hair.

"You have beautiful hair," she remarked, and this time the smile did reach her eyes as reflected in the mirror.

"Thank you."

"I think all it needs is a product application and tongs to reintroduce the waves that have flattened out a little. Is that what you were hoping for?"

"Yes. Something like that. I was wondering if you could recommend a conditioner?"

Now Rachel had hit the right note, Esther waxed lyrical about the exclusive hair products on offer in the salon and how best to manage her hair so it would always shine. Rachel was actually quite enjoying the lesson, but felt that she needed to move the conversation on to Keith Bird. The trouble was, how?

Pierre brought her tea and placed it on the ledge in front of Rachel, giving her a wink before he left.

"Do you have a hairdresser back home?" asked Esther.

*Eureka!* "I don't have a regular anymore. I moved to Leicester from London earlier this year, so I haven't found anyone like Keith, my old stylist."

Rachel had been studying Esther's face for a reaction and got one: a twitch of her mouth and the characteristic flick of the hair she had picked up on earlier.

"I think we're done," Esther snapped.

Ignoring her, Rachel continued, "Keith is a wonderful stylist. He has a salon in Knightsbridge, just down the road from where I used to live. I pleaded with him to open up a new one in Leicester, but no joy. Have you ever worked in London?"

"I did, earlier in my career," Esther's reply was terse as she waited for Rachel to get up while clearing her brushes and comb away.

"Didn't we have a Keith from London in here on boarding day?" Pierre had been showing another passenger to the chair next to Rachel's. "Rather handsome, as I remember."

"I don't recall anyone of that name," snapped Esther, whose face was flushing more with every passing second.

"That's funny, I thought you knew him. He gave that impression. He was here for an interview." Pierre told Rachel, "Keith Bird, I think his name was."

"That's him!" Rachel said enthusiastically. "Keith Bird. Funny he should apply for a job on a cruise ship, though."

"Why is that funny?" Esther asked indignantly.

"Sorry, I didn't mean to offend. It's just that he runs a successful salon in London. Having said that, a lot of businesses are struggling, and competition is fierce. Perhaps his business isn't doing as well as it was. I haven't seen him in months."

"Why didn't he get the job?" asked Pierre, clearly enjoying the discomfort he had detected in his boss.

"How do you know he didn't?" she snapped.

"Well, he's not here, is he? He told me he'd come back and buy me a drink if he got it because I gave him a few tips."

"A few tips about what?"

Now it was Pierre's turn to redden. "That would be telling." He showed the teeth again, held his head up high and returned to reception.

"Small world, isn't it?" said Rachel. "Fancy Keith being on board the same ship. I must track him down and say hello."

"I don't think that will be possible." Esther's shoulders dropped.

"I'll ask at guest services, see if they can put me in touch—"

"I don't... never mind, they'll tell you anyway. Unfortunately, Mr Bird had an accident on the night he boarded and drowned."

Esther's knees buckled. Rachel stood up.

"Are you all right? Let me help you." She took an arm firmly and led the paling salon manager to the office. A few stylists stared open-mouthed before returning their attention to their clients.

"You really don't have to manhandle me in this way. I'm quite all right."

"I thought you were going to faint. Can I get you a glass of water? I'm trained in first aid."

Esther seemed too tired to argue and nodded to the water dispenser in the corner of her office. Rachel filled a paper cup and handed it to her.

"I apologise if I upset you. That must have been an awful shock. Did you know Keith?"

"A long time ago. We worked together for a while, that's all. It upset me to hear of his untimely death. And now—"

"Now what?"

"And now I really must get on. Thank you for the water. The salon will add the style to your bill, Mrs Jacobi-Prince." The officious Esther had returned, and unless Rachel was going to tell her why she was quizzing her, it was time to leave.

Pierre was waiting eagerly at reception. "She does know your Mr Bird. They were lovers in the past."

"Oh, how do you know that? Although I'm not surprised, he always was a ladies' man."

Pierre showed the white teeth once more. "I got that impression. Such a waste – I would have liked to show him a good time." He tilted his head back and laughed a dirty laugh. "She turned him down for the job. I saw him later

103

on boarding day and he told me she still resented him for breaking her heart. I told him that was news to me – I didn't think she had one." Pierre laughed again, and Rachel chuckled politely at the joke.

"Thank you, Pierre. I'd better find my husband before he sends out a search team." She signed the chit Pierre placed in front of her and tucked the unrequited love motive away in her head as she left the rather toxic salon.

\*\*\*

Rachel tracked Carlos down just as he was about to enter the restaurant for lunch.

"I thought I'd find you here," she laughed.

"Darling! I called into our suite, but you were out. I see where to." His eyes shone. "You've had your hair done."

"How observant you are, Mr Jacobi-Prince."

"When it comes to you I am, Mrs Jacobi-Prince." He took her hand and they walked through to the table for two. The waiter, Gerome, pulled out the seat for her.

"Welcome back, beautiful lady." He winked towards Carlos, who grinned in appreciation. "May I say, your hair looks adorable."

"Goodness, you're not the only one who's observant," she remarked to Carlos.

"It appears not. I believe I have a rival." His eyes twinkled. "Have you had a good morning, darling? I hope you didn't tell me you were going to the salon and I forgot."

"No, it was a spur-of-the-moment thing. The salon's amazing – I've not been there before. Not lacking in friction, though."

They chatted happily over lunch and ate far too much food for Rachel, who would have preferred a salad from the buffet, but Carlos enjoyed relaxed eating. *It must be something to do with his Italian heritage*, she mused. He was anglicised in many ways, but there were some parts of his background he clung to – something she agreed he should do, and it made him even more attractive, in her opinion.

After they had eaten, Carlos studied her.

"What?"

"I love the plait on top of your hair and the soft waves suit you. I love everything about you, truth be told, except…"

His steely gaze held hers and her heart pounded.

"Except what?"

"Except your determination to involve yourself in every murder that happens on board this ship. Which, by the way, should have its name changed to *Killer Queen*." He roared at his own joke.

"Don't mention that to Waverley. Anyway, I don't know what you mean."

"Male intuition. And… your reaction just gave you away."

"That's not fair." She kicked his shins under the table.

"Ouch! I hope my bride will not use me for karate practice anytime soon. You forget, I know you, Rachel. From the minute I heard about that cousin of Sarah's dying, I feared you would involve yourself, especially as it turns out to be murder. Plus, you don't fool me. He was a hairdresser, and you take a rare excursion to a hairdressing salon this morning. Not that I disapprove of the results, but I assume the two things are connected?"

Rachel huffed. "Who told you it was murder?"

"I'm a private investigator. I know these things," he teased.

"Who told you?"

"I ran into Jason. We had an interesting conversation about the women in our lives, as it happens. I think 'stubborn' and 'self-willed' were mentioned."

"Pot calling kettle," she retorted. "How's he taken it?"

"He's worried about Sarah but determined to get to the bottom of it. I said I would help in any way I could, but he insisted we didn't get involved while on honeymoon. Something I would have agreed with, but—"

"Oh, Carlos, thank you. I thought you'd be angry, and yes, the salon visit is related. Keith and the salon manager were an item well over eight years ago, but according to a chatty and rather spiteful receptionist, there's still resentment on her side. Esther – the manager – told me the breakup was mutual, but Pierre – the receptionist – spoke to Keith after she refused to give him a job, and

Keith had insisted she'd never forgiven him for breaking her heart."

"My, my. And you found all this out over a cup of coffee and a hairstyle. How come she told you anything?"

She grinned. "Tea, actually. She had a funny turn when I mentioned that Keith had been my stylist when I lived in London."

"You didn't tell me that."

"That's because he wasn't. I haven't seen Keith since schooldays – a white lie."

"White lie, black lie, still a lie. I don't understand that expression."

She was about to protest, but noticed the twinkle in his gorgeous brown eyes.

"When you look at me like that, I want to be in your arms forever," she conceded.

"Good to know I have some charm left after two days of marriage."

They laughed as they sipped their coffee.

"You'll be interested to hear that Jason is going to re-interview the group of friends your hairdresser was on holiday with. I expect you'll be able to worm your way into the group somehow. In fact, I've got an idea on that score."

Carlos explained they could catch Keith's group at the captain's cocktail party that evening and offer their condolences. She agreed it was an inspired plan.

"Will they be there, do you think?" she asked.

"From what you tell me, they'll be pleased to be, especially as free drink's involved. Remember they tried to gate crash our reception."

"So you're not cross with me?"

"No, I'm not cross." Carlos's handsome features clouded all of a sudden and a glumness came over him.

"Rachel, I have something to tell you and you're not going to like it."

# Chapter 11

Carlos gripped Rachel's hand tightly as they strolled around the outside decks. She had said little in response to his revelation, and he understood her need to think. He'd kept a secret from her, and he wondered if she would come to terms with it. This was not the honeymoon he'd dreamed of.

Finally, she spoke. "Why didn't you tell me this before?" Her watery blue eyes gazed up at him.

How could he answer? He didn't know himself why he had mentioned nothing about that period of his life. Now he had to face his new wife and come up with an explanation.

"It was all so long ago. I guess it was something I wanted to forget."

"Not that long ago, though, was it? I've been trying to remember where I'd seen her before. Was she on the cruise when we first met?"

He slapped his head in disgust. How could he have been so stupid? He hadn't even realised that Rachel had seen them together back then. If he wasn't careful, this situation could spiral out of control.

"Rachel, I'd forgotten she was on board that time, but what I've just told you happened years before I met you. Believe me." He didn't feel he could say anything further without incriminating himself and telling the whole story.

"And now you tell me she just happens to be on the same cruise as you, again. That she's in trouble and you want to help, but you can't – or won't – tell me what kind of trouble or why you need to be the one to help. On our honeymoon."

Her shrill voice had drawn the attention of one or two people passing by. Carlos winced.

"Shall we go back to the suite and talk about this?"

"What's there to talk about? You've met an old flame, you lied to me when I asked who she was, and now she has a problem and needs your help. I tell you what, you go and help her. I'm going for a lie down." She snatched her hand away from his and glared at him. The hurt in her eyes tore him in two. "I trusted you." She turned away in disgust and stormed off.

Carlos's heavy heart threatened to burst at the disappointment that had filled the eyes he adored, and the weight in his stomach ripped at his insides. He should have told Rachel; they had agreed to tell each other about past liaisons, but had he done so, he would have had to tell her about things he hadn't been at liberty to reveal. Telling her now would create an even bigger rift.

He stared out at the ocean, wondering whether he should run after her. The happiest moments of his life were spiralling out of control into an unbidden nightmare.

Carlos shook his head free of despondency. This situation would get sorted, one way or another; the love he and Rachel shared was bigger than this and she'd come round once she'd had time to think.

Carlos made his way downstairs to the Piano Lounge where the woman responsible for his present woes sat waiting.

"You've told her, then?"

"I've told her you and I were in a relationship once and now you're in trouble and need help."

"Wow! I wasn't expecting that one. So I guess she's annoyed."

"You could put it that way, yes."

"Well at least the part about me being in trouble is true. Why didn't you tell her I was just a friend?"

"Because she'd want to know more. This way, she's annoyed about me keeping our fictional relationship from her. That will stop her digging for now, but I wouldn't bank on it for too long, especially as she remembers you from the last Med cruise."

"Wow! She is observant. In that case, you should tell her everything."

"I refuse to put her in danger, Helena." But Carlos knew his Italian friend was right. He squared his shoulders and stared resolutely at the woman he had bonded with during a time in his life that he had thought he'd put behind him.

"Carlos, if it's any consolation, I don't want either of you to be in danger, but there's no-one else I can trust. As I told you yesterday, we have a leak in the department, and if I don't find out who that is, there will be many more lives at stake. I can't call this in, but I have to stop this racket."

Carlos exhaled. He knew there was more at stake than his and Rachel's lives, but he couldn't help wanting to protect his new bride from any fallout now that he'd agreed to assist Helena. Why was he so protective? Rachel could take care of herself, he knew that, but he still had difficulty accepting it.

"At least she's got a murder to investigate," he said grimly.

Helena raised her eyebrows. "A what?"

"A cousin of her best friend Sarah Bradshaw – she's a nurse on the ship – was murdered the day we boarded."

"The nurse?"

"No. The nurse's cousin. Keep up, Helena."

"What an interesting couple you make. It's a shame you can't introduce us. I'd love to meet the woman who won your heart and caused you to give up working for the agency."

He shrugged. "Maybe I would have given up anyway. I hated leading a double life. Don't you ever tire of it?"

"Not really. You know me; I'm loyal to our country like my father and grandfather before me. It's in my blood."

Carlos also felt loyalty to his birth country, having been recruited to the External Intelligence and Security Agency as a young man while working for the British army, and later, the SAS. He'd engaged in joint covert operations in the past, but had decided not to do any more work for either body after meeting Rachel; he hadn't wanted to lie to her, and now he'd done just that because his past had caught up with him.

Helena believed Italy was in imminent danger of multiple terrorist attacks and was on board the *Coral Queen* to track down a vital link in the chain. She had explained to him that her boss had sent her on the mission alone because she suspected there was someone inside the agency feeding information into the terrorist network. Helena was the longest serving officer in the team and above suspicion.

Carlos had resisted getting involved initially, deeply torn between love for his new wife and love for his birth country. But he owed Helena his life, and that of his family. During a mission that went wrong, she had rescued him from a warehouse after he had become isolated. Later, Helena had discovered a rogue arms dealer who he had thwarted planned to kill his parents. She tracked the arms dealer down and removed him from circulation on a trumped-up charge of drug dealing.

"Your family would be very proud of you."

Helena beamed. "Thank you. I am sorry for dragging you into this, Carlos, and for causing you trouble. When I saw you come aboard, I couldn't believe my luck. Sorry it had to be your honeymoon, though."

Carlos looked up at the ceiling. "Me too, but I'm in now, so we had better get this over with as soon as possible if I'm going to save my new marriage. And when it's over, I will tell Rachel everything."

"I understand. It's the right thing to do. The agency won't come after you for that. They will owe you one."

"Again." He smirked, and she raised her brandy glass in salute.

"Again."

# Chapter 12

After stomping around the suite for an hour, unable to get any sleep, Rachel tried reasoning with herself. Her honeymoon was degenerating into a soap opera and, if she didn't do something soon, it would be ruined.

She replayed the conversation with Carlos repeatedly, but it made little sense. That was, unless he still held a torch for the mysterious Helena. Rachel believed him when he told her the relationship had ended some years before they had met on her first Mediterranean cruise, although she couldn't understand why Helena would have been on board back then.

In her shock and anger, she hadn't demanded to know why the woman just happened to be aboard the same ship at the same time as they'd chosen for their honeymoon. Surely he hadn't invited her? No, that didn't fit with the conversation she'd overheard yesterday morning. She could bring herself to believe that one encounter was coincidence, but it was stretching it to believe Helena had appeared by chance on two cruises at the same time as Carlos, years apart. Perhaps she was stalking him.

Now that was a possibility. What if Helena had invented the alleged trouble she was in to get Carlos's attention? This thought disturbed her.

Was it only yesterday that she had woken up in a sublime state? Now she felt the polar opposite, but being rational at heart, she needed to come to her senses. The only thing Carlos was guilty of was omitting to tell her of a woman he had been in love with in the past. Maybe it still hurt, or perhaps it had been a genuine oversight. She hadn't given him a chance to explain once he had revealed he was going to involve himself in the mystery difficulty the woman had got herself into.

*I don't think you'd be so bothered if Helena wasn't so beautiful,* her alter ego taunted.

"Shut up," she replied out loud. Not being one to sulk forever, she decided it was time to park the Carlos thing and get on with investigating the death of Keith Bird. At least that would help her regain a sense of control.

She picked up the phone and dialled Sarah's room.

"Hello, Sarah. Do you fancy afternoon tea in Creams?" Sarah sounded surprised by the invitation, but agreed.

Ten minutes later, Rachel found a quiet table at the rear of the café, their favourite daytime haunt. Sarah joined her a few minutes after she had arrived. To look at Rachel's friend, no-one would realise she was the chief suspect in a murder investigation.

They ordered tea and cakes from the patisserie menu.

"Have you uncovered something?" Sarah asked.

"Not really. I met with the hairdressing salon manager."

"Esther Jarvis? Why?"

"It turns out she interviewed Keith for a job on the day he died. Also, they had been in a relationship some years back, and rumour has it she's still bitter about the breakup. Although she denies it, Keith apparently broke her heart."

Sarah shook her head in astonishment. "Rachel Prince, you're a genius at getting people to open up. You would make an exceptional nurse."

"Oh no I wouldn't. But I do make an outstanding detective."

"I don't suppose she confessed to killing my cousin?"

"Sorry, no. I don't even suspect she had anything to do with it, really. It's too far-fetched to imagine that she would kill him after all this time. She'd punished him enough by turning out to be the boss and then refusing to give him the job. That would have hurt his pride. I'm sure that's all there is to it. It has to be one of the company he came on board with. We just need to know who, why and how."

"Any leads on that front?"

"Not yet. That's where you come in. I want you to join me at the cocktail party tonight so we can strike up a conversation with them."

"How do you know they'll be there?"

"Just a hunch. They had no qualms about gate crashing my reception, so I can't see them turning down free cocktails."

Sarah nodded as she bit her lip, the only sign she was still worried.

"Surgery will be finished by then so I'll meet you there afterwards. What about Carlos?"

Rachel blinked back the tears that had been threatening to fall all afternoon.

"Rachel! Whatever's the matter?"

The waiter arrived with tea and cakes, allowing her a few moments to get a grip. After he left, she took a bite of the cinnamon slice.

"Mm. This is divine."

Sarah drank some tea and took a bite of her lemon drizzle cake.

"And?"

"Oh, nothing unusual, really," Rachel couldn't hide the sarcasm in her voice. "That woman I told you about that Carlos has been meeting with. It seems she's an old flame. She was at our reception. Not invited by me – I thought she was with his friends and family, then I thought he was planning a surprise for me. I don't suppose you got around to finding out whether she was working for the hospitality team, but you needn't bother now."

Sarah dropped her gaze. "Sorry…"

Rachel continued, "So now the woman is in a spot of bother, and has convinced Carlos he's the only one that can help."

"Have you met her yet?"

"Nope. He pretended she didn't exist at first. I saw them talking at the reception and he changed the subject when I asked who she was. Then I heard him on the phone yesterday morning, speaking Italian with someone in a secret call. After I left you yesterday lunchtime, I went to find him and spotted them in deep conversation on the Lido Deck. Then I convinced myself he was organising a surprise for me and was hoping you would confirm she was the new assistant cruise director."

Sarah shook her head, looking guilty again.

"Don't worry. I realise you've been busy since this morning. He dropped the bombshell after lunch."

Rachel felt better for getting it all out in the open. All this sneaking around just wasn't like Carlos. That he was sneaking on their honeymoon made it far worse.

"Carlos loves you, Rachel, of that I'm certain. If he's keeping something from you, he'll have good reason. I've never met a man more devoted."

"Thanks, Sarah. I have just about come to that conclusion myself, but I don't have to like it."

Sarah laughed. "That's for sure. Where is he now?"

"No idea. I stormed off in a huff."

Sarah raised her eyebrows. "He's likely waiting for you in your suite. Perhaps you'd better put him out of his misery."

"Certainly not. He's not getting off that lightly. I'm having more tea. How about you?"

\*\*\*

Sarah found it hard to concentrate on her work after the encounter with Andrew Farmer the previous night and the fright she'd had when he returned. The discovery that he had been looking at her cousin's notes had put her on edge, and her imagination had played all sorts of tricks on her. As it was, he'd only returned to ask for a new inhaler as he'd used up the one he'd brought with him.

She arrived at the medical centre early to finish typing up records from her on-call visits the previous night. The day had flown by and there hadn't been time. She was about to close down the computer and join the others for coffee prior to evening surgery when she had a thought.

She typed a name into the search engine.

"Okay, let's get to know more about you, Andrew Farmer."

The screen came alive with articles and many images of the bulldog-faced man she had treated the night before. His bright blond hair and dark green eyes did nothing to lessen the doglike caricature Sarah had created in her mind.

In fact, when she read in one article that the man had been barking orders to his constituents, it made her chuckle.

"What's funny?" Bernard joined her in the consulting room, placing a coffee on the desk she was sitting at.

"Nothing really. I'm looking up an MP I treated last night."

"Military police?"

"No, member of parliament. A government minister."

Bernard pulled up a chair and shuffled around to see the screen. "He looks like a—"

"Bulldog," she laughed.

"I was going to say fat dog, but yes, I see what you mean. Anyway, why are you interested in him?"

Sarah explained about the encounter the previous evening and how she suspected Farmer had looked up Keith's details while she was out of the room.

"He could have been trying to find your cousin's room number."

"Yes, that's what Rachel says, but I'm not so sure. If you met him, you would agree with me. He's smarmy."

"I agree he looks that way from these photos. He's involved in some high-stakes deals, by the looks of things. In my country, such things always involve bribes, especially when construction's involved. Look, he seems to be jet-setting all over the world, too."

"The Philippines doesn't have a monopoly on bribes; I think you might be on to something there. His sons are at private schools. That Mercedes isn't cheap, either."

They perused more images of the seemingly wealthy housing minister via multiple search engines and news headlines. There was nothing linking him to corruption, but that didn't mean he wasn't involved in it. He just hadn't been caught.

"How did he know your cousin?"

"He says Keith was his stylist, which could be true. Keith bragged about the high-class clients he got in the salon and some of the secrets he could tell. What if it was one of those secrets that got him killed?"

"The Brits don't go around killing people because they find out a secret. In my country that might happen, and in Africa maybe, but surely not yours?" Bernard slapped his hand on his thigh. "Come on, drink up. You've got surgery. Brigitte's on call. Are you going to the captain's bash?"

Sarah nodded. "Are you in this room, then?"

"Yep. You're next door."

Sarah got up. "See you in a while."

She remained deep in thought as she fired up the computer in the next room. She often read about corruption in top places, and there were killings related to gang and turf wars in parts of the UK, but Bernard was right. As far as she was aware, political scandal might be commonplace back home, but murder to cover up such scandals would be unheard of.

She inhaled before going to the waiting room.

"Mr Holloway?"

She recognised the enormous frame of the man she'd met a few times over the past week. He had been staying with Keith's parents and Keith had said he was his investor, but she hadn't been paying much attention. She sighed. The regret at ignoring her cousin recently and the argument on the night he'd died remained a weight on her shoulders. Now, here was another reminder of that regret. Were all Keith's friends going to come into her consulting room during this cruise?

She grimaced, then composed herself.

"Please take a seat," she pulled the chair reserved for larger passengers towards her desk. "What can I do for you?"

Maxwell Holloway tapped his fingers on the table while she brought up his limited medical record. Age forty-one, high blood pressure – unsurprising, considering his weight. He didn't speak, so she turned her attention back towards him as his finger tapping became more pronounced. His clothing was 1980s casual: polo shirt with turned-up collar underneath a pastel-blue suit with rolled-up jacket sleeves. She didn't look, but assumed he was wearing loafers on his feet.

"Mr Holloway?"

His round face lifted, but he avoided eye contact.

"You're Keith's cousin." The man's timid voice seemed odd coming from one so large.

"I'm Nurse Bradshaw. Now, what can I do for you?" she asked again, impatience getting the better of her.

"I need a blood pressure check. I've been getting headaches recently."

Sarah reached for the bariatric blood pressure cuff.

"Please could you remove your jacket, Mr Holloway?" she asked.

"Call me Max. We met in Brodthorpe. I was staying with your cousin. I'm sorry for your loss."

Sarah smiled. "And I'm sorry for yours. I understand you were in business with Keith."

Max removed his jacket, temporarily preventing him from tapping his fingers on her desk. "We were business partners. I invested in the Knightsbridge salon. It seems I'll have to take over now that he's—"

Sarah applied the blood pressure cuff. "I just need to listen with my stethoscope for a minute," she advised and applied the diaphragm over his brachial artery while pumping up the cuff. After she released the cuff, she typed the figure onto his record.

"Don't you have electronic equipment to check blood pressures?" he asked, eyeing the machine on her desk.

"Sometimes old-fashioned is best," she said, not having the heart to tell him that the electronic recordings in extreme obesity weren't as accurate. "Your blood pressure is normal, Max. If the headaches continue, please come again. I hope to see you at the captain's cocktail party later. Perhaps we can talk more about Keith then."

He stood up and, in a low, secretive whisper, said, "And perhaps you can tell me what you were arguing about."

Sarah gazed at the closed door for a few moments after Max left, wondering what that parting shot had been about.

# Chapter 13

Captain Jenson greeted people at the entrance of the Coral Ballroom, welcoming passengers for the cocktail party. Each group or individual stopped for a photoshoot with the captain and a brief chat. Occasionally officers had to intervene to move the overenthusiastic ones along so the next could get through.

The captain beamed as Rachel and Carlos joined him.

"Congratulation, Mrs Jacobi-Prince. It's a pleasure to have you on board again, along with the usual intrigue."

Rachel's jaw dropped at the direct reference to the murder, although no-one listening in would have guessed what the captain had meant.

"Good to be here, Captain," she replied.

The captain continued, "May I say, you look stunning this evening, Rachel. You're a very lucky man, Mr Jacobi-Prince."

"Indeed, I am." Carlos smiled adoringly at his wife.

After a brief conversation and the compulsory photoshoot, they made their way through the crowds to where Sarah was standing with the group of people Rachel wanted to meet.

"Rachel! You look radiant tonight," Sarah exclaimed.

"Thank you."

"You look good as well, Carlos." Sarah kissed him on the cheek. Rachel couldn't agree more. Carlos in a tuxedo took her breath away. His handsome features and confidence, along with the fact that he was a private investigator, always reminded her of James Bond. Women turned their heads to gaze at him and Rachel felt proud.

She had gone to substantial lengths with dressing to impress, choosing a turquoise cocktail dress with a handkerchief hem, and she'd lightly applied makeup to her face and eyes. She hoped that and her restyled hair, which had cost a small fortune, would remind him of their first cruise, when he hadn't been able to take his eyes off her.

It was working.

"Let me introduce you to Keith's friends." Sarah turned towards the quartet. "Rachel knew Keith when we were growing up and was sad to hear the news of his death." She addressed the comment to no-one in particular.

Rachel assessed the gang of four, as she'd nicknamed them, to help her remember who each one was. This was the first time she'd met them in person.

"This is Jean." Jean's eyes were fixed firmly on Carlos as Sarah spoke. "These are my friends, Rachel and Carlos."

"Charmed," said Carlos, taking the rapidly blushing woman's hand.

*The accountant*, thought Rachel. *And the gossip.* Jean was pretty, with flaming red hair and leaf-green eyes that hadn't moved from Carlos. The woman immediately dominated his attention, plumping out the full lips covered in bright red lipstick that matched her hair. She wore a short white tight-fitting cocktail dress and held a half-empty glass.

Sarah continued the introductions. "This is Max, Keith's business partner."

Max took Rachel's hand with a firm grip. She had to look up at him as he was about six-four, built like a truck and massively obese. He avoided eye contact, but she could make out the round pale-blue-grey eyes that were ogling Sarah.

"Pleased to meet you," he said without taking his eyes off Sarah. "I was at your wedding."

Rachel almost spluttered something rude about that fact, but held back in time, remembering what she was trying to do.

"I hope you enjoyed it," she said instead.

"I saw you there," Carlos intervened before she could change her mind and go on to say something rude anyway.

*How could anyone have missed him? It's not like Max would have just blended in.*

"This is Luke, Max's cousin," Sarah continued.

"Nice to meet you, lovey."

The lanky man before Rachel couldn't have been more different to his cousin in size or manner. He released her hand quickly as he too was mesmerised by Carlos.

"Well hello, lovey. Aren't you a sight for sore eyes?" Rachel wondered for a moment whether the affable extrovert knew Carlos.

"Ignore him. He's always like this, a show-off if ever there was one. I'm Duncan. I was close to Keith. *Very* close."

Rachel took Duncan's hand. He was older than Keith, and she remembered from what Waverley had told her he was a senior stylist at the salon in Knightsbridge.

"Oh, I expect you knew him better than I did then. We'd lost touch until recently. He came to Brodthorpe where we both grew up about a week ago, and then to our wedding. I think you were all there, too, but we didn't get the opportunity to chat. This is Carlos."

She turned to her right. Jean had accosted poor Carlos again.

"We were at the wedding. Lovely ceremony. Keith said your dad was the vicar. He welcomed us and asked about each one of us. He's friendly, your dad." Duncan shot a quick glare at Sarah, who was trying to pull Jean away from Carlos. "We tried to attend your reception, but Keith's cousin was having none of it."

"Yes, Sarah told me. I'm pleased you liked my father." Rachel took a different tack. "So you were close to Keith. Were you an item?"

Duncan dropped his head, exposing a thinning patch at the centre of his overly moussed curly black hair. "I'd like to say yes, but no. We were best friends, but nothing like that. Keith liked the ladies."

"Did he like anyone in particular?"

"Not recently. He picked them up and put them down, if you know what I mean? He said he was hoping to catch up with an old flame when he went home for one last fling before she got—" Duncan's hand went to his mouth. "OMG! That was you, wasn't it? I'm sorry. No offence."

Rachel pursed her lips to hide the annoyance over Keith's lie. They had never been an item.

"None taken, but Keith and I were only ever friends." Even friends was pushing it. "There was never anything between us."

"He was attractive, though. He could have had any woman or man he chose. It's a shame he wasn't bi."

"Looks aren't everything. Keith wasn't my type." *He would never have had this woman.* Rachel gritted her teeth and held back the angst rising in her throat.

Sarah disentangled Jean from Carlos and they joined her. Carlos shook Duncan's hand, gaining another fan.

"I see you made up," Sarah whispered to Rachel.

"Sort of. I've called a truce for now, but I will find out what's really going on between him and the Greek goddess."

"I thought she was Italian?"

"She is, but I can't get Aphrodite out of my mind."

"Don't go there, Rachel. She's an old friend, that's all. I tell you what, while you're busy on my case, I'll ask Jason to find out what Carlos's helping her with."

"Now why didn't I think of that? Brilliant idea. Ask him to find out if the trouble she's in is real."

"Why? Do you think she's making it up?"

"I'm not certain. For all I know she could be stalking him."

Sarah raised a concerned eyebrow. "Okay. It won't do Jason any harm to have something else to focus on to keep him out of danger. Captain Jenson's told Waverley Jason has to stay out of the investigation."

"Which we knew would happen," said Rachel.

"But Jason's not listening. I'm worried about him, so sending him after Carlos will benefit both of us. I'll ask him to do a background check on Helena while he's at it."

Rachel nodded. "You're right, and a background search wouldn't go amiss as long as Carlos doesn't find out. It will also mean I don't have to see Carlos and Aphrodite together again."

Both women laughed and Rachel felt better. Carlos joined them, putting his arm around her waist. Max followed, fixing his gaze on Sarah.

"Were you really the last person to see Keith alive?"

Sarah stepped back, but then pulled herself to her full height and squared up to the big man.

"No. That would have been his killer."

"Of course, sorry." Max backed down and hung his head. "What were you arguing about?"

"I can't remember. It was a family thing. Keith could be highly strung."

"I can second that," said Luke, sidling alongside Carlos. "One minute he was all smiles and flirting, the next he was throwing things around the salon."

"He never threw anything around the salon," Duncan jumped in. "You were never in the salon, so how would you know?"

"Don't be touchy, lovey. Just saying, that's all."

"He was unpredictable, liked to yell." Jean the gossip would not miss out on her say – or on Carlos, as she shoved Luke out of the way.

"What would you know? Your job was accounts. I was the one in the salon with him every day and I can guarantee he threw nothing," retorted Duncan.

"He lost his rag sometimes, though. You have to admit that," said Max. "I wasn't there often, but I heard talk."

"See!" exclaimed Jean, triumphantly.

"So who would want him dead?" asked Rachel.

The reaction was immediate, each member of the group looking to the others. Clearly they all suspected that one of them could be the killer.

Luke spoke first. "We don't know. The security chief only told us today that his death wasn't an accident. I'm still reeling about it, to be honest. We were good friends."

"He was my best friend, so I didn't do it," said Duncan.

"Why are you so interested anyway, lovey?" asked Luke. "You hadn't seen him in years."

"And how did you know that?" asked Sarah.

"Keith mentioned it when he was going up north."

Rachel chuckled at the prospect of Hertfordshire being considered 'up north'.

"It could have been the Mafia."

Rachel and Sarah stared wide-eyed at Luke.

*Where did that come from?*

"Don't be silly," Max cut in.

"I'm not," retorted Luke. "He used to go on about the Mafia when we were in training. Told me I had to beware of who I did business with."

"That was to keep you out of his way." Duncan patted Luke on the shoulder before turning back to Rachel. "Keith made stuff up to impress. Most of it was bravado."

Rachel remembered Keith referring to his one salon as a 'hairdressing chain' on her wedding day. That and past experience confirmed Duncan's assessment.

"Whatever happened, it wasn't one of us who killed him. We all know who saw him last, and we all know about the bitter argument. You need to be looking closer to home." Jean shot daggers at Sarah, challenging her to deny it.

"And who was it who witnessed the argument?" Sarah shot back. "Perhaps *they* were the last person to see my cousin alive."

Jean flushed as all eyes turned towards her.

Max cupped his chin. "The nurse's right, Jean. You should be careful who you go around accusing. It might backfire."

"Jean's not capable of murder. We all know she was secretly in love with the boss," said Duncan.

"Really?" Luke asked.

Rachel watched on as the group of friends rapidly moved away from murder to the latest piece of juicy gossip. Duncan and Luke then debated which of the passengers would benefit from a new hairstyle. Jean remained fixated with Carlos, while Max seemed to be developing a crush on Sarah. He hadn't taken his eyes off her since leaping to her defence.

Rachel moved to the periphery and helped herself to another cocktail from a plump waiter trying to escape a large group of men who had already had too much to drink. He flashed her an appreciative smile and offered Carlos and the rest of the group the remaining drinks on his tray, much to the dismay of the rowdy group.

"Hey, you, fat boy, bring some more back here," a large man with a South African accent yelled at the waiter. Carlos bristled at the outright offensiveness, and Rachel sensed a row brewing. He didn't need to intervene, though, as Jason and a few of the other security guards had obviously been monitoring the drunks.

"You'll have to leave now, sir. We don't tolerate insults to passengers or crew."

The man was about to argue, but Jason's jaw sharpened.

"Sorry, mate. No offence meant. I didn't mean anything."

"No, sir," said Jason in a tone that warned the obnoxious man he meant business. "This way, sir." Jason pointed the man towards an exit while the other three security guards ensured the rest of his group followed.

With the scene over, Rachel realised she was standing alone as the ruckus had pushed her to one side. The waiter scowled after the men before turning to Rachel, grinning. She tried to head back towards Carlos, but was intercepted by Esther Jarvis.

"Ah, Mrs Jacobi-Prince. How's the hair?"

"It feels fantastic, thank you. I almost didn't recognise you out of context. Your dress is beautiful." The salon manager wore a low-cut red evening gown showing off her long neck and a beautiful shell necklace.

"The advantages of working on a cruise ship. We can buy designer clothes at reasonable prices. Just a word of warning."

"Oh?"

"Don't believe everything Pierre tells you. He's a gossip. Nothing more. He told me about your conversation. I've done a little research into you. You have quite a reputation on board this ship. If I were you, I'd stay out of matters that don't concern you." The flintlike stare held Rachel's gaze.

"That sounds rather like a threat." Rachel held her ground. *Two can play the staring game.*

"Take it more as a warning. Keith was no longer in my league, but he was in some sort of trouble, and history tells me that it would be safer for all concerned if you stayed out of it."

"What sort of trouble?"

Esther's eyes flashed daggers. "Women like you just never give up, do you?" was her parting shot.

Rachel gawped after the woman in disbelief as Esther marched off.

Sarah appeared at her side. "What was that all about?"

"I don't understand. I may have just been warned off."

"Off what?"

"Something to do with Keith being in trouble. Esther knows something and I have every intention of finding out what, and also why your salon manager has it in for me."

"Rachel, you've got that look in your eye."

"Look? What look?"

# Chapter 14

Rachel tried to lie still in bed. Unable to sleep, she was mulling over the suspects who might have killed Keith Bird. Although she didn't like Jean Sutton, she couldn't think of a good reason for the woman to have killed her employer. As his accountant, Jean would have been privy to Keith's financial details, so they could reveal motive and be a good place to start. The problem was, if Duncan was to be believed, Jean had a crush on her employer. Whether the crime was financially motivated or down to love, Rachel didn't know, but either way, it wouldn't make sense for Jean to kill him if she fancied him.

Carlos turned over. "Can't you sleep either?"

"Sorry. Did I wake you?"

"No, I've been thinking about your case."

"Not the case of goddess Helena, then?" she snapped, but regretted it immediately.

Carlos sat up in bed and stroked her hair. "Darling, I'm sorry I didn't tell you about her, but you have to believe that I love you with all my heart."

Rachel knew she was being silly, but couldn't help herself. "So you said."

He turned her head, so she was looking at him. "*Tesoro,*" his voice cracked, "you mean the world to me." He kissed her tenderly. She tried to harden her heart, but soon yielded.

"I suppose resistance is futile," she laughed.

"You know it is. As we're awake, shall I make coffee, then we can compare notes?"

She looked at the time displayed on the bottom of the television: 2am.

"Why not?" she said, sitting up.

They sipped coffee and Rachel broached the subject, despite promising herself she wouldn't. "What sort of trouble is your Helena in? Perhaps we can help each other."

"She doesn't want anyone to know. I'm sorry, Rachel. You must trust me on this one." He pecked her nose. "Now, what did you think of those four friends of Keith's? That woman definitely has it in for Sarah."

"You mean Jean, the one who wouldn't detach her hand from your arm?" Rachel giggled as Carlos shrugged. "You're right, she's keen to lay the blame on Sarah. I've been thinking about her a lot. If she's not hiding anything, she might believe Sarah killed him."

"She obviously doesn't know Sarah. But that doesn't mean she's not innocent herself."

"Perhaps she's an excellent actress. I haven't decided which yet, but I believe she had a thing for Keith, which makes it unlikely that she's our murderer."

"Oh, I don't know. A woman spurned and all that," he laughed.

Rachel chuckled. "Well she's coming after you next!"

"I don't think so."

"Don't pretend you hadn't noticed her attention. Luke was just as bad."

Carlos drank more coffee. "How could I notice another woman with you before my eyes?"

Rachel thumped his arm, then mused for a moment. "That Max Holloway is a shifty character. Gives me the creeps."

"He struck me as a gentle giant, but you've got good intuition where people are concerned. What would be his motive?"

Rachel rubbed her forehead. "That's just it. I don't really have any motives yet. It appears he was a silent investor in the Knightsbridge salon. According to Waverley, and Duncan confirmed it, he's stinking rich so doesn't need to work. Unlike his cousin, Luke, who has a trail of business failures behind him. Keith's salon attracted the wealthy and famous, so it could have something to do with that. What if Max discovered Keith was involved in some underhand dealing?"

"But wouldn't he just have challenged Keith or pulled his money out?"

"Most people would, but he comes across as inadequate, needy. He might have been jealous, or what if Keith had something on him and was blackmailing him? That might be the actual reason he invested in the business. Then he got tired. Waverley told me that he's financing this holiday. Why would he go along with that?"

"But if he's as rich as you say, that might be small change."

"People can tire of being used, Carlos." There was an edge to her voice that she couldn't hold back. The Helena thing was still rattling her.

Carlos either missed it or chose to ignore it. "You could be right there. Blackmail makes sense and being used would get to a person. That's a good start. He's strong enough to have whacked Keith over the head with a fire extinguisher with ease. Jean Sutton told me – when I managed to stop her from flirting, that is – that Max followed Keith around like a bloodhound."

Rachel yawned. "I'll do some more digging on Max Holloway, but for now, I need to get some sleep. You too. It's our first stop tomorrow."

Carlos pulled her into his arms. "Goodnight, *Tesoro*."

\*\*\*

It was good to be on land after two full sea days. The Bay of Biscay had been calmer than at any other time Rachel had crossed previously, and the weather was glorious as she and Carlos walked down the steps leading off the ship. The forecast was for thirty-two degrees centigrade.

They followed groups of excited passengers all vying to get ahead of the crowds. Buses lined up ready to take people on organised tours, so everyone scattered once they hit the tarmac.

A photographer stopped Rachel and offered to take a photo. Usually she would have refused, but as it was their honeymoon, she agreed. They had decided to join a hop-on, hop-off bus rather than a formal tour so they could enjoy Cadiz at leisure. Buses stopped off outside the port all day long and transported cruise passengers on a circuit.

Carlos studied the route map once they'd sat down at the front of the open-topped upper deck. Rachel rested her knees on the front shelf and put on her sunglasses. She had dressed for the heat in white knee-length shorts and a sky-blue vest top, her long blonde mane tied in a ponytail. The sunlight caressed her wedding ring, causing it to sparkle alongside the diamond engagement ring. It was time to relax and enjoy a day in the sun.

"Where would you like to get off?" Carlos asked.

Rachel leaned across to glance at the map. "Let's head to the beach. I want to feel sand beneath my feet and fresh sea air on my face."

"As opposed to the un-fresh sea air on the way here."

She grinned. "You know what I mean, I want to take my first beach walk with my deliciously attractive husband."

"Well, in that case, first stop, Santa Maria Beach. We can walk on to the next stop at Victoria Beach. Then, if you don't mind, I'd like to walk through the Botanical Garden on the way back."

Rachel took his arm in hers and rested her head on his shoulder. This was what she had been looking forward to through the months of hard work and doubts leading up to the wedding. She still had to pinch herself when she looked at Carlos. He was irresistible in his khaki shorts and black vest top. His biceps protruded and oozed strength. She glanced down at his olive-brown knees. The earlier application of sun cream caused them to glisten in the sun. Rachel couldn't believe this man had committed his life to her and she to him.

Carlos interrupted her dreamy reverie when he grabbed her hand.

"Come on, gorgeous. We're here."

They leapt off the bus with enthusiasm and Carlos raced her down the steps to the beach.

"What's the hurry?" she giggled.

"You said you wanted to walk on the beach with a handsome hunk. Here we are." He pulled her into his arms and kissed her tenderly. "Mm. You taste good."

"Come on, you, or we'll get nowhere." She bent down and took off her sandals. The sand felt glorious beneath her feet, soft and tender just like the man she watched removing his own sandals. The salt in the air breathed new life into her lungs, and a slight breeze made the heat less sticky. It couldn't have been more perfect. Not a cloud in the sky.

They walked towards the shore where the waves lapped against the sand as each gentle movement broke into a line of foam. Carlos walked into the sea up to his knees and splashed her as she followed. They soaked each other, playing in the water, giggling and messing around with carefree abandon, straying further and further until the sea reached their waists.

"Oh, I wish we'd brought swimming gear," she complained.

"You go ahead, you're soaked anyway. I'll take your bag and the backpack and sit on the beach, waiting for you like the good husband I am."

"Okay, you're on."

Feeling reckless, Rachel turned around and swam out to sea. She was a powerful swimmer, so went quite a way out before turning around again. Carlos was lying down on the beach and she waved, but he wasn't looking. She smiled.

*He must be tired after our late-night talk.*

Deciding it was time to head back, she had to swim hard against an undercurrent that wanted to veer her right and stop her return, but it didn't bother her. It slowed her down, though. Finally, she got to where her feet could touch the ground beneath the waves and walked the scant distance to where Carlos was still lying on his stomach.

"Hey, sleepyhead!" she called. He didn't respond, lying slumped over his rucksack with his vest off. "Stop playing, Carlos. I'm ready for a drink." She leaned down and shook him.

Something wasn't right; his skin felt clammy. Struggling to breathe, she knelt down beside him and pulled him on to his back. Panic ripped through her.

"Carlos, wake up!" Then she saw the sandy blood running from his chest.

# Chapter 15

Carlos groaned and put his hand to his chest, the blood seeping between his fingertips as Rachel knelt down to grab him, overcome with joy that he was alive.

"Darling, thank God. I thought you were dead. You terrified me. What happened?" Words tumbled from her mouth as she tried to take in the sight. There was blood staining the sand and Carlos's vest, which he must have held against his chest.

Carlos sat up, dazed, and rubbed his head. "Sorry. I must have fainted. It's the heat."

"Not to mention this," she pointed to his shoulder. "I need to get you to a hospital."

"No. No hospital, they'll ask questions."

Rachel took a towel from the rucksack. She poured water over the wound and removed as much sand as she could before drying it.

"That... that looks like a bullet wound to me." Her voice trembled as she spoke. "Please, Carlos, let me call an ambulance and get you to a hospital."

"It's okay. It looks worse than it is. The bullet went through the rucksack strap, look." He held up the rucksack and she saw a hole billowing straight through the strap that would have been sitting on his right shoulder. "I don't think it's a deep wound. It was just so hot when I sat down to cover it, I either fainted or fell asleep."

Rachel stared, aghast. "Carlos, you're talking as if you've scratched yourself on a thorn. For heaven's sake, you've been shot!" Her voice sounded screechy in her own ears, but she couldn't help herself. How could he be so calm? "Were you robbed? We need to call the police and get you to a hospital."

Carlos pulled her from crouching to a sitting position while holding the towel over his wound. "Rachel, listen. It wasn't a robbery. Someone took a shot at me. We can't go to the police or the hospital because I don't know who we can trust. These people have eyes and ears everywhere."

Rachel stared at her husband in disbelief. "You're scaring me. What people? Is this to do with one of your cases?"

He pulled the second water bottle out of the rucksack and looked around as if checking whether they were being watched. Rachel followed his gaze, her hair dripping seawater down her back, but all she could see were tourists and locals milling around.

The beach was busier now than when she had gone for her swim. A couple settled themselves down on towels for the day nearby while their children blew up inflatables to take into the water. A group she recognised from the cruise were walking further along the beach, shouting and having fun. Two older couples strolled hand in hand. No-one looked their way.

In the distance, she could see the busy road and seafront cafés, booths and shops. A hop-on, hop-off bus stopped, and she watched as passengers got off and some got on. The sky was a serene blue and the heat burned down on her back, drying her clothes.

Carlos gulped down the water before speaking again.

"Rachel, trust me. We need to get something to cover this wound and buy me a shirt, and then head back to the ship. Once we've set sail this evening, I'll call Jack Waverley and Dr Bentley and get this thing removed. It's not deep." He smiled grimly. "If I were a soldier in Afghanistan, I'd pull it out myself."

"You're not in Afghanistan, you're in Spain. This is ridiculous, but I'll do what you ask on the condition you tell me what this is all about."

"Agreed. But for now, would you get me a fresh shirt? I'll wait here."

"No way! I'm not leaving you here. Put my towel over your shoulder. I'll soak your towel in seawater and you can hold that against the wound. We'll walk up to the road and you can sit on a bench while I go into the nearest tourist shop for a shirt and chemist for dressings."

Rachel helped him up. He was wobbly, and as the colour drained from his face, she wondered if he would pass out again. His old army training kicked in and she watched as he stooped down and took some deep breaths, then he finished the bottle of water. She would need to get him something salty to eat.

Hauling the rucksack up from the beach, she threw it on to her back and kicked dry sand over the blood that had congealed into a lumpy pile. Thankfully the sand was dry and the process didn't take too long. Worried children might wander over and find the blood, she dug a trench leading down to the sea where the waves lapped, watching as water ran into the gulley and made its way to where the blood was. Satisfied it wouldn't take too long for any traces of blood to be washed away, she hurried after Carlos, who had started a slow walk towards the roadside.

"That was clever," he said, taking her arm.

She grinned. "I'm not just a pretty face."

"You don't need to tell me. I married you for your brains, not your looks!"

"If you weren't injured, I'd jab you in the side for that. Right. What colour shirt – blood red?"

They both laughed, causing Carlos to wince and put his left hand tight over his right shoulder. With every step they took, Rachel knew he was playing down the extent of the gunshot wound and the pain he was in. Her mind reeled with thoughts about what was going on and why he felt he couldn't trust the Spanish authorities, but she wouldn't interrogate him now. She could read him well enough to realise that he was doing his best to stay conscious.

After what seemed like an eternity, they arrived at the road, and Rachel punched the air when she saw an older couple get up from the bench right in front of them and wander off in the direction of the hop-on stop. Carlos sat down and Rachel took her handbag from the rucksack, plonking the sack next to him on the right-hand side.

"At least if anyone sits down, they'll be on your good side. I'll be as quick as I can, but first I will get you salt and sugar."

The smell of fried salami reached her nostrils and she went to a nearby takeaway to grab him a Spanish hot dog and a can of cola.

"Thank you," he said as she handed them to him.

Rachel rushed across the road and bought him a black t-shirt with Cadiz emblazoned on the front. Moving out to the road again, she could see Carlos still eating. After a quick glance round, she was satisfied that no-one was watching him, so she headed off in search of a pharmacy.

She had walked all the way along the seafront with no success, so headed off the main road. Ten minutes later, she found a pharmacy and bought a first aid kit rather than trying to explain what it was she needed to an assistant who didn't speak English. She also bought an electrolyte mix.

Once outside again, she jogged back to where she had left Carlos, but slowed down when she saw someone sitting next to him. The familiar wavy black hair filled her with rage. As she approached, it was impossible to interpret their intense conversation, as it was in Italian.

"I see you found company." Rachel couldn't help being terse. They jumped, startled at her appearance.

Helena was even prettier close up, her olive-brown skin and protruding cheekbones emphasising the round brown eyes. She smiled sheepishly.

"Good to meet you at last, Rachel."

The woman's genuine tone was disarming, but Rachel would not give in that easily.

"As I've only known of your existence for two days, I can't join you in the 'at last' part." She knew she was being childish and hated herself for it.

Carlos groaned, causing her to disengage her eyes from Helena.

"I thought I'd keep your husband safe until you returned." Helena shot a grin at Carlos. "Sorry, Carlos. I'll leave you to it then. I have some things to do."

Rachel watched the back of the woman's body as she strolled away.

"She doesn't lack confidence, does she?" she snapped as she turned her attention to Carlos. Removing the rucksack from the seat and placing it on the ground, she opened the first aid kit. "Good job I did my refresher recently. Funnily enough, though, it didn't include removing bullets. Should I try with these?" She held up a pair of plastic forceps included in the box.

"I'd rather we wait."

"Joke, Carlos." She kissed him on his pale cheek. He shivered.

"Sorry. I'm feeling cold."

Blast! The last thing she needed was for him to go into shock right now.

"Here, take this." She handed him the electrolyte mix she'd spotted in the pharmacy.

"Ah, electrolytes. Good thinking,"

"As I said before, I'm not just—"

"A pretty face," he finished.

She found the pressure dressing and pressed it hard against the wound. Carlos winced.

"Hold that for a minute." He dutifully pressed while she mixed the electrolyte salts into half a bottle of water so he could drink it down. Afterwards, she taped the dressing in place, and then applied the bandage that came with the kit. Once satisfied with her handiwork, she pulled the t-shirt from the bag.

"To remind you never to stray away from me," she laughed as she showed him the emblazoned shirt.

"Really?"

"It was that or Meatloaf. Don't ask me – they didn't have much in black, and the red ones were for kids. I could have got you white, but as you want to pretend you're not injured—"

151

"All right, all right, I've got the message." He smiled as some colour returned to his face.

"I don't think we'll get on board without giving the game away, you know," she warned.

"Why? I can pretend to be okay. No problem."

"There's something you've overlooked."

"What's that?"

"The minor problem of a piece of metal in your right shoulder and the detector you have to walk through to board."

He paled again. "You're right. What are we going to do?"

"It's already done," she teased.

"You called Jack Waverley?"

"No way! He wouldn't have let you on without an explanation, and if you remember, I don't have one to give."

"Sorry." He looked down at his feet, then back towards her. "Sarah then?"

"Wrong again." She was enjoying this. "For a private investigator, you're not great at guessing."

He rubbed his head. "Jason?"

"Yep. He was the only one I knew who would overlook your cloak-and-dagger reasons for not wanting to visit a hospital. Not that he understood, but he trusts you. He agreed when I told him you would fill him and Waverley in later."

Carlos nodded. "I don't mind letting Jason in on the story. I was going to tell him anyway."

Rachel didn't know whether to be pleased or annoyed that he would share with Jason what he hadn't yet shared with her. She saw a bus pull into the hop-on stop on the opposite side of the road.

"Time to go."

"Sorry for ruining our day out."

"No problem. At least we got to walk on the beach hand in hand and I got to take a swim in the Spanish sea." She hauled the rucksack from the ground as Carlos handed her the towels to pack. "Yuck! Shame we have to take these, but who knows what blood-borne disease you're carrying."

He raised his eyebrows in protest, but said nothing, taking her arm instead.

There was a queue getting on the bus, so they could take their time crossing the road. They took their seats downstairs near to the back.

"I really am sorry, Rachel."

Rachel was barely listening. Her mind was a whirr of all kinds of thoughts, impatient to know what was going on. It annoyed her that her honeymoon was being ruined by crime, but the real annoyance was the all too frequent popping up of the troublesome Helena.

# Chapter 16

The bus stopped outside the port entrance, where they followed the returning crowds into the terminal. After showing their cards to the security guard at the entrance, they found a bench in the terminal building. By this time, Carlos's colour was back to normal.

"I'll call Jason and let him know we're here."

After making the call and putting the phone back in her shorts pocket, Rachel turned to Carlos.

"He'll call us in fifteen minutes. Shall I get some coffee?"

Carlos nodded and Rachel headed towards a café to get drinks. As soon as the smell of food hit her, she realised she hadn't eaten since breakfast and was famished. There wasn't much choice of the takeaway variety, so she bought two panini filled with salami and salad.

Turning around with the food and drinks, she was exasperated to see the irritating sight of Helena once again sitting next to her husband. Huffing heavily, she headed purposefully towards the couple, almost taking someone out in the process.

"Hey, watch where you're going!"

She turned to say sorry and came face-to-face with a woman in officers' whites.

"I'm so sorry. I wasn't looking."

The woman's face was wild, but nowhere near as wild as the hair. Rachel suspected from Sarah's description that she had run into the new doctor who was giving the medical team so much trouble.

"Clearly!" the woman snorted before turning and marching off in disgust. Rachel giggled as she noticed the grouchy doctor bumping into an elderly gentleman who gave her a piece of his mind. The scene was like something from a skit where a situation goes from bad to worse in minutes.

Smiling to herself, Rachel had temporarily forgotten why she was in such a hurry. She turned back to head towards Carlos, who was now minus his new fashion accessory. She was pleased the coffees hadn't spilt, but she almost threw his at him.

"What's the matter?" he asked.

"Don't give me that. What was she doing here?"

Her 'don't you dare deny it' look worked and stopped his imminent protest.

"Do you mean Helena?"

"Unless you have a string of ex-lovers stalking you, yes, I mean her." Rachel couldn't bring herself to acknowledge her rival's name.

"Jealousy doesn't suit you, Rachel." Carlos grinned, sheepishly.

"And sneaking around behind my back doesn't suit you," she snapped.

"I'm not—" He thought better of continuing with the protestation. "Darling, I think you're hungry. Why don't you eat that," he nodded towards the panini, "and have some coffee?"

Now he was being infuriatingly reasonable. She bit into the panini with such venom, she surprised herself.

They spent the next few minutes in silence, both eating, drinking and musing on how to break the ice that had developed between them. Rachel felt guilty for being annoyed with her injured husband and was angry with herself for her overreaction. But was it?

"Just tell me, Carlos, why that woman is around every time I turn my back. Are you still attracted to her?"

At that moment, the phone vibrated in her pocket. The relief on Carlos's face was obvious.

She snapped into the phone, "Yes."

"It's me, Jason. I'm ready. Come to the crew entrance about halfway down the length of the ship. I've just relieved a colleague for ten minutes."

"Right." She threw the waste from their drinks in a recycling bin and picked up the rucksack again with a sigh.

"We need to go. We don't have long," she told Carlos shortly. The ache in her heart was overwhelming her. Everything she had worried about before marrying him was coming true. The dread of Carlos turning into a carbon copy of her ex fiancé, Robert, could now be a reality. Her steps were heavy as they walked towards the crew entrance.

Jason's cheery face brightened her mood a little. He kissed her on the cheek before addressing Carlos.

"You've been in the wars, mate."

"Thanks for doing this, Jason. For reasons I'll go into later, I couldn't go to a hospital on land. I have to avoid police involvement."

"I'm sure you've got your reasons, but we'd better get you through sharpish. Evan will be back in a few minutes. Give me your cards and I'll scan you through. You head through the metal detector. It'll beep, but I'm here, so don't worry."

Sure enough, the metal detector sounded as Carlos went through. Under normal circumstances, security would send him back to remove anything from his pockets and search him, but these weren't normal circumstances.

Jason cursed.

"What?" asked Rachel.

"It's refusing to swipe you in because you're not crew. Hang on. I need to exit this program and go into the passenger screen." Jason sounded calm, but Rachel recognised the signs of anxiety as he worked quickly, worried his colleague might return at any minute.

"Phew," he said at last. "You're in. Now look, you'll need to turn left on to the M1, and then walk straight down. There's an entrance to the passenger decks through door 8. If anyone stops you, act drunk or confused and tell them you took a wrong turn. If they give you trouble, tell them you're friends of mine and that you were looking for me. They'll radio me and I'll confirm. Get going. I'll catch up with you both later. Just a few more hours before we sail. Do you want me to send Sarah up?"

Rachel considered it for a moment. "No. I don't want to involve her if we end up having to turn the ship around due to my husband's stubborn behaviour. It's enough we've had to involve you."

She hurried Carlos away, leaving Jason to make his way back into the crew program. She heard a crowd greeting him as they arrived back from shore leave. Carlos walked faster than he'd walked since she'd found him slumped in the sand. At least the food had helped, she reassured herself, and most likely the caffeine burst.

The M1, as the crew called the principal route below decks that ran the length and breadth of the ship with multiple exits to various areas unknown to passengers, was busy with crew shuffling fresh supplies through in large containers. Below the M1 were the crew cabins, tiny rooms that two to four crew members shared. She had been below stairs occasionally as part of her previous investigations.

They passed a few members of crew who weren't pushing heavy trolleys, but they were too busy going about their daily tasks to be bothered about a couple of stray passengers. From a distance, Rachel and Carlos might have been mistaken for members of the entertainment staff or musicians returning from shore leave. Crew came and went at regular intervals, and with over fifteen hundred members, they wouldn't all know each other.

Once they were on the passenger decks, Rachel relaxed. They took a lift to deck fifteen and their suite. Once inside, she realised how much her heart had been pounding. She hoped they were doing the right thing and that she wasn't putting Carlos's life at risk by following his wishes.

He went straight into the bathroom and ran a shower. She followed him in, horrified to see blood had soaked through the dressing. He took the t-shirt off and let her remove the dressing while he sat on the side of the bath. Pulling her to him, he kissed her tenderly.

"I love you, Rachel. There is no other woman for me. Please believe me."

She stared into his adoring eyes and recognised he was telling the truth.

"I do believe you. But Carlos, I'm really worried about this gunshot wound right now. Are you certain we're doing the right thing? I couldn't bear it if anything happened to you."

He stroked her hair as she helped him off with the rest of his clothes.

"It will be okay. I promise."

"Is this person who took a shot at you likely to be on board?" she asked, realising that this thought had been nagging at the back of her mind since she found him.

"I don't think so," he replied as he kissed her forehead.

Rachel left him to shower. Returning to their suite, she picked up the phone.

"Mario, would you bring us a pot of filtered coffee, please?"

Rachel flung open the balcony doors to let fresh air into the room and took some deep breaths. Air conditioning was no substitute for genuine air, although port air wasn't always the most conducive to good health.

Mario brought in the coffee and put it on the table. "I hope you had a good day out, Mrs Rachel."

"We took a walk along the beach. The sand here is delightful," she replied. "Did you get any time off?"

"Not today, but I'm going ashore tomorrow. I enjoy Malaga very much. Can I get you anything else, Mrs Rachel?"

"No, thank you."

She poured the coffees as Carlos came out of the bathroom with a towel round his waist.

"Could you tape this for me?"

He was holding a flannel against the wound. "Great idea for a pressure dressing," she approved. He winced again as she replaced the newly rinsed bandage around his chest and shoulder. "That should keep it in place until we set sail," she said. "Now, Mr Jacobi-Prince, come and get some coffee. I want an explanation."

Carlos acquiesced and sat down on the sofa.

"Close the doors, please."

She sighed heavily. "This really is becoming too much. Why can't I just take a normal cruise like anyone else? Not only do I have a murder to investigate, I have a husband behaving like he's a spy."

His silence was deafening as she picked up the coffee he had poured.

"You will not like this."

"I already don't like it, so I don't imagine it can get any worse."

"Okay, here goes." He took a sip of coffee. "It involves Helena."

Rachel's mouth dropped open. He was right; she didn't like this start, not one little bit. Why hadn't she suspected that it involved his newly found appendage? She had been convinced it was something to do with his most recent case. "I see," was all she could bring herself to say. But she didn't see at all. Who was this woman who was taking all her husband's attention, and was now responsible for him being shot on a beach in Cadiz, of all places?

"Helena works for the Italian Government. That's how we met."

"Are you telling me she's a spy? Don't tell me you are too, Carlos, not now. Not after we're married." Her voice had risen several decibels.

"No. I stopped working for them after I met you and was never an employee. They recruited me to do jobs for them when I worked in the army, and later as part of the SAS when the two governments worked joint operations, because I had joint citizenship. My contact in Italy was Helena. Not her actual name."

"Of course not. Why would it be? There was I, imagining she was just a deranged stalker." Rachel couldn't disguise the sarcasm in her voice. "So she works for the Italian equivalent of MI6, you mean?"

"Yes, *Agenzia Informazioni e Sicurezza Esterna*, AISE for short. After I left the army and worked as a private investigator, they would call me from time to time to help. I never told you because I left soon after we met. I fell in love with you and didn't want to live that kind of risky life. Being a PI can be dangerous enough."

"I get it now. You were also doing a job for them on our first cruise, as well as protecting Marjorie. That's why you were talking to her back then. Am I close?"

"Yes. I was working with Helena on that cruise, watching one couple while she was watching another. We successfully broke up a small terrorist cell."

"Now it makes sense. No wonder you were so distracted on that cruise."

The irony of the situation hit her, and she burst into fits of giggles.

"What are you laughing at?"

"I'm remembering how you failed to keep Marjorie safe and everyone thought it was because you were too besotted with me. All the time, you were breaking up a terrorist cell. My bungling, incompetent private detective was not that at all. I'd always wondered about that – I've seen you at work since then and you have never been that remiss again. If I hadn't been so attracted to you, I would have thought you a poor detective."

"Ah, but Rachel, I *was* besotted with you. Still am." He kissed her tenderly as the phone in their room rang.

Carlos picked it up. "It's Helena," he mouthed.

Her heart sank.

# Chapter 17

Sarah couldn't get Andrew Farmer out of her mind. She was convinced he was somehow involved in the death of her cousin, but why? As far as she could tell from news headlines, Farmer was responsible for big construction deals involving vast sums of money. What if Keith had heard something that incriminated him?

"It's usually about money," she said out loud. She needed to find the link between this man and her cousin to help Rachel discover what had happened.

She pulled up Farmer's record again, more convinced than ever that the asthma attack hadn't been genuine. He could have triggered it himself, she mused, but why would he take such a risk? That part made little sense, so Rachel could be right about him just taking a peek to find out which room Keith was in. No great crime there. To convince Rachel he was the culprit, Sarah needed evidence.

After closing up the medical centre, Sarah headed towards guest services. Most of her colleagues were on shore leave, apart from the obnoxious Brillo, who seemed determined to create tension in the team. She hoped they wouldn't be called to attend anyone who fell ill together. Brillo didn't have much time for the nurses; she behaved as if they didn't exist, and huffed and puffed every time any of them had to ask her about anything, as if their very presence was beneath her pay grade. Bernard was more determined than ever to give the new doctor one of his lethal stinger cocktails, his kill-or-cure remedy.

"It helped relax Gwen, remember," he had reminded Sarah when she suggested it was a bad idea.

"Gwen wasn't obnoxious, though, was she?"

"Well something has to be done, or Brigitte is likely to inject her with something just as lethal as my stinger and I won't be held responsible. Plus, Rachel will have another murder on her hands."

Sarah thought about the unpleasant doctor as she approached guest services. She was pleased to see the friendly Ben on duty.

"Ben, could you check for me whether a Mr Andrew Farmer is still on board? I saw him in surgery a couple of nights ago and need to check something with him."

He picked up his phone. "Anything for you, Nurse Bradshaw." As well as being helpful, Ben had a penchant for flirting with anyone in a skirt. She smiled.

"Hi, Cissy, Ben here. Can you tell me if a Mr Andrew Farmer's booked on a trip today?... Yes, love, me too... He is? Where?... Thank you, love. I owe you."

Ben put the phone down.

"He's booked on a sightseeing tour of Cadiz; it includes the Jerez horse show and sherry tasting, so he'll be out all day. Sorry."

Sarah tried to hide her glee. "Never mind. I can catch up with him tonight. It's not important, just a loose end I wanted to tie up." She had another thought. "I don't suppose you could check he has left the ship? Sometimes passengers don't join their trips, do they?"

"You're right. Hang on." Ben picked up his phone again and called down to security. Following a brief flirtation with the female security guard, he shook his head.

"Sorry. He's definitely off ship."

"Oh well. I'm sure I can find something else to do."

"I would if I were you. That new doctor's on the warpath again. In fact, she was down here looking for a passenger around ten minutes ago. She was in a right mood; not at all like Alex, is she? We miss Greta terribly."

Alex Romano, the previous junior doctor, had left with Greta, who'd worked in guest services, to get married in Italy.

"Not as much as we miss Alex." She blew out her cheeks. Brillo Sin was not the replacement the team had been hoping for. "Can you remember who it was Dr Sin was trying to trace?"

"No. She spoke to Fran, who got an earful for not being able to help. I was dealing with another passenger. Thank God."

Sarah nodded and thanked Ben for his help. Was she really brave enough to go through with what she had in mind, or should she wait for Rachel? No, she had to take the opportunity that presented itself.

She made her way up to deck eight. The room attendants would have finished for the morning, so now was the best time. With her heart threatening to leap from her chest, she walked casually along the deck, having checked the corridor was clear.

One thing about port days was the ship was quiet. She was on call, but the likelihood of being called was slim, unless a member of crew fell ill or had an accident. A small percentage of passengers stayed on board, but would be at lunch or sunbathing.

She paused outside the executive suite to steady her nerves. Her hand shook as she entered the universal swipe key that all medical staff carried in case of emergency.

The room was dark, as the stateroom attendant had closed the curtains to block out the sun. She hoped the butler was also off-duty as she stood with her back to the door, taking deep breaths.

*Now's the time to exit before you break every rule in the book, Bradshaw.* If anyone caught her, she would lose her job. But, she reasoned, this was about justice. *I need to know what happened to Keith and whether it involves this man.*

She crossed the room. Using the light from a small gap between the heavy drapes to find her way, she pulled them open just enough to brighten up the room.

Executive suites were luxurious, and this was one of the largest. It oozed extravagance. Taking a quick glance around the lounge, she noticed a bar with half-empty spirit bottles. There were a few papers on the coffee table, which she leafed through, but they were nothing more than cruise itineraries and newsletters.

The bedroom revealed nothing new. She bit her lip, wondering what the heck she was doing.

*Have you lost your marbles, Sarah Bradshaw?* she asked herself.

Last stop, which should have been the first stop, was the safe. It opened on the second attempt. Jason had told her that passengers almost always used birthdate combinations and warned her never to do so if she was travelling.

The safe revealed a passport, designer watch, a box containing a row of gold cufflinks and a large stash of cash piled to one side. She let out a low whistle.

*Wow! He's well off, that's for sure.*

There were some documents on the bottom shelf that she was about to reach for when she heard a swipe key being pushed in the door. She quickly closed the safe, leaving it unlocked, and crawled under the bed to hide.

Holding her breath, she heard someone enter the outer room. She was sure the person would hear her breathing if they came into the bedroom. Perhaps it was housekeeping or a delivery of fruit.

She waited. It was hot and stuffy under the bed. The only redeeming feature was that the housekeeping team kept the rooms spotless, so there was no dust to make her cough.

Her heart sank as she heard the drapes being pulled back and the balcony doors opened. Farmer must have skipped his trip and returned to the ship early. This excursion was turning into a nightmare. She lay as still as she possibly could, deliberating over her next move. Would she be able to dash out while he was on the balcony?

She crawled from under the bed, but quickly scuttled back when there was a knock at the door. The bedroom door was wide open. She saw Farmer's legs as he crossed the room.

"What's this about? I was supposed to be out today," he grumbled.

Sarah could just make out male legs wearing shorts following Farmer back out to the balcony.

"I had to see you. It's important."

Sarah thought she recognised the other man's voice, but the conversation trailed off as they both headed out on to the balcony, deep in conversation. She just made out the visitor saying, "It will not be easy, I can tell you," before they moved out of earshot.

The balcony wasn't in direct view of the suite door, so Sarah decided this was her chance. As she made her move, her leg caught on the buckle of a suitcase and she had to stifle a gasp. While trying to check the damage, she hit her head on the underside of the bed.

"Ouch," she muttered, unable to stop herself. She froze for a moment, holding her breath. Muffled voices remained on the balcony. Feeling more calm, she crept out from under the bed and pushed the suitcase back in place. It felt heavy, as if still full.

Stopping for a moment to check the voices were still out on the balcony, she slowly heaved the suitcase out and opened it. Her mouth dropped open as she gawped at the contents. Then Sarah pushed the suitcase back under the bed and took her chance to exit.

# Chapter 18

"She likes you, says you're feisty."

That was the last thing Carlos said to her before going into the bedroom, lying down and falling asleep.

Rachel waited for the ship to sail while mulling the day over in her head. As she had got no further explanation from Carlos before he crashed, she tried to work things out for herself. Her husband had been a spy and not told her, and now he had got himself involved in someone else's mission and ended up being shot for it.

Memories of her broken heart flooded back and how she'd fallen for her now-husband on the rebound once she'd decided he wasn't a would-be assassin. She wondered whether it had all been a pipe dream and she had made the wrong choice by marrying him.

She shook that thought out of her head, almost cricking her neck. This was getting her nowhere. Time to move on to what she could control: the investigation into the murder of Keith Bird.

What she had surmised so far was that people didn't like Keith. He had been handsome, that was undeniable, but he'd lacked sincerity. This had been confirmed through her meeting with Esther Jarvis. He would have hated being turned down for a job, which explained why he would gossip with Pierre rather than lose face.

But why was he looking for a job in the first place, and why had he wanted to speak with her? The answers to these questions might hold the key to why someone killed him. She would ask Waverley what his team had found in the dead man's room once she had Carlos sorted.

At that moment, the captain's voice came over the loudspeaker, announcing they were preparing for departure to the next port. A noise came from the bedroom. Carlos must be waking up.

"Coffee?" she called.

No answer.

She walked into the bedroom, "Would you like some cof—?"

Her voice trailed off and panic seized her chest as she saw her husband lying on the floor. Rushing over, she put her hand on his arm to wake him. He was burning up.

"I'm freezing," he said, trembling.

"You need to get to the infirmary, now."

She picked up the phone and requested urgent medical assistance, telling the operator her husband had collapsed with a high fever. Then she mopped his brow and put a pillow under his head on the floor, covering him with a blanket and stroking him.

"Oh, Carlos, why didn't you let me take you to hospital?"

Moments later, Sarah arrived, with Bernard and Dr Bentley following behind. Rachel stepped back and let them work.

"It's a gunshot wound," she said as Dr Bentley removed the blood-soaked flannel from Carlos's chest.

Dr Bentley, ever the professional, didn't bat an eyelid. "Right, team, let's get him stable. Bernard, put a line in. Then we'll get him down to the infirmary."

"Yes, sir."

Bernard went to work, inserting a drip line into Carlos's arm. Sarah radioed down for a stretcher, then checked pulse and blood pressure. Rachel stood by helplessly, watching as her husband lost consciousness and the medics went about their tasks.

The door flew open and the new doctor arrived with Brigitte. Sarah re-covered the wound.

"Infected abscess," Dr Bentley said. "He's rigoring; we need to get him down to the infirmary."

Brillo Sin glared at Rachel, clearly remembering their earlier encounter. She then barked orders at Bernard, Brigitte and Sarah to get Carlos on the stretcher. Dr Bentley tutted and muttered something under his breath.

"We'll take it from here. You go and prepare for evening surgery, Doctor Sin. Tell Gwen to open up the infirmary," he commanded.

Rachel observed the redness rising up the formidable Dr Sin's neck. Her hair appeared to stand out even more and she didn't move.

"Now, Doctor." Dr Bentley raised his voice and glared at the new doctor, who turned on her heels with a huff and left the room.

"Not a word about this to anyone. Understand? At least not until we know what happened and why Mr Jacobi isn't already in hospital. I'm assuming he wasn't shot on board this ship."

He directed the rhetorical question at Rachel. She shook her head.

"Will he be all right?"

"He's in danger of septic shock, but don't worry, Rachel. We'll sort him."

Rachel ran down the stairs with Sarah, as there wasn't enough room in the service lift for all of them.

"Shot? Rachel, please tell me this has nothing to do with Keith's death."

"No, Sarah, it doesn't. Will he really be all right?"

"He's in shock, but Graham is the best in the business. We'll get him sorted. We have to keep it from Brillo, though. She's likely to report it to the port authorities. That woman is not to be trusted."

"Will she believe the abscess thing?"

"No reason why she shouldn't. It's not unusual, and more common than a gunshot wound."

They arrived at the infirmary and Rachel sat outside while the team went to work. Brigitte came out a few minutes later.

"Dr Bentley's getting him ready for surgery. We've stabilised him and given him an intravenous dose of penicillin." She put her hand on Rachel's shoulder. "I'd better do evening surgery."

Gwen came out moments later. "Come on, Rachel. Let's get some coffee. They will be a little while, but he's stabilising. We need to talk." The senior nurse tilted her head towards her office while pointing to one of the consulting rooms. "We don't want any prying ears," she whispered.

Rachel collapsed in a chair in Gwen's office and put her head in her hands.

"I should have made him go to hospital. If anything happens to him, I'll never forgive myself."

Gwen poured a cup of freshly percolated coffee and joined Rachel on the sofa. Her office was where the medical staff had meetings and chilled out with debriefs after a hard day's work.

"Don't talk like that. He'll be fine. Look, I hope you don't mind, but I've called the security chief down. Graham insisted."

"No, it was only to be expected." *I'd rather not do it now*, she thought, *but there will never be a good time.*

175

"Raggie can keep our new doctor occupied with a full surgery. She has to cover Graham's on-call anyway, so that should keep her out of our way. She doesn't socialise with us, so shouldn't come in here. Wonders why I don't fetch and carry for her, but that's another story. Drink up."

Waverley burst into the room, breathless.

"I'm so sorry, Rachel. Is he all right?"

"He's in surgery," Gwen answered for her. "Sit down, Chief. We need to fill you in."

"You said someone attacked him. Who?"

"That's not quite what happened, but I didn't want to say anything over the phone. Coffee?"

Waverley nodded and took a seat. "Why do I feel I won't like what I hear? Don't tell me you've been sticking your nose in where it's not welcome again, Rachel?"

Gwen handed Waverley a coffee and rejoined Rachel. "If you can just stay calm for a moment, I'll tell you. Carlos has been shot."

Waverley's neck reddened, followed by his face. He coughed loudly.

"Shot?"

"Please, Chief, keep your voice down. We don't want the new doctor to hear about this."

"But how? It's almost impossible for anyone to get a gun aboard this ship."

"It happened in Cadiz," said Rachel, speaking for the first time. "On the beach, and I don't think it would have been a gun. More likely a rifle. Carlos didn't see who it was."

Waverley coughed again, took a deep breath and gulped the coffee.

"I hate to state the obvious, but why isn't he in hospital? What are the Spanish police doing about it? I'll call them and give them a piece of my mind. We need to keep this out of the papers."

"Chief, please. This isn't helping," said Gwen. "The bullet is being removed by Graham now. The police weren't informed and Carlos didn't visit a hospital while ashore."

Waverley rubbed the almost invisible hair from his forehead while he registered what was being said.

"He can't have a bullet in his body. We would have picked it up on our metal detectors."

At that moment, Jason walked in. "About that, sir."

Waverley coughed for the third time in as many minutes, his face changing from red to purple. Rachel felt sure his blood pressure couldn't take much more.

"Shall I start from the beginning?" suggested Rachel to Waverley, whose angry glare told her he was about to rip Jason to shreds. Gwen poured another coffee for Jason, who sat in the other chair.

"Perhaps that would be best," she said, her calm voice diffusing the tension filling the air.

"Carlos and I were on the beach. It was gorgeous. We both had this urge to walk hand-in-hand along the sand."

Rachel smiled at the only happy memory from their day ashore. Waverley sighed heavily, obviously wanting her to get to the point, but said nothing.

"I went in for a swim while Carlos stayed with our belongings. When I came out, I found him slumped over on his stomach. I thought he was sleeping until I saw he was bleeding. He was pale and had lost some blood, but woke up – I think he must have fainted. He said it was the heat. Anyway—"

"So why didn't you call for help?"

Rachel glared up at Waverley through tear-filled eyes.

"Don't you think I wanted to? He wouldn't let me. Said he didn't trust anyone and that we had to get back to the ship. I agreed on condition he told me – and you – what was going on."

"Did he tell you?" asked Gwen.

"He started to, but the phone in our room rang. To be honest, I'm not sure how much I'm allowed to tell you of what I know, which isn't very much. After the phone call, he went to lie down until the ship set sail. He fell asleep. The next time I heard him was when he fell to the floor. He was burning up."

Ignoring her distress, Waverley spoke, his voice sharp.

"To convince me to keep the port authorities out of this, you will have to tell me everything, young lady."

Rachel could see from Waverley's darkening eyes he meant what he said.

"He's been meeting with someone on board ship. Don't ask me their name, because I don't know." If Helena worked for the Italian government, Rachel had no intention of blowing her cover, particularly as Carlos was going out of his way to help her. "He's been helping this person with an investigation."

"So it has nothing to do with the Keith Bird case?"

Rachel sighed. "Chief, I've had a really gruelling day and my husband is near death, so could you please let me finish?"

Waverley coughed. "Sorry."

"I don't know what the investigation entails other than it might involve a criminal gang working out of Italy. He wasn't sure whether the gang's tentacles reached Spain or whether there might be corruption within the local police force."

"Sounds far-fetched to me."

"Nevertheless, I trust my husband's judgement and therefore followed his wishes."

"And how did you rope Goodridge here in on this? Through Sarah, I suppose."

"Sarah knows nothing about it, sir. The first she will have heard would have been just now. Rachel called me, explained what had happened and what Carlos had said. I agreed to help as long as he spoke to you once we set sail. He's ex-forces, sir. You know how it is. I didn't enjoy doing it," Jason jutted his determined chin forward, "so sack me if you like, sir, but I would do it again."

"All right, Goodridge. No need for the melodramatics. I can't blame you for helping a friend and ex-serviceman, as long as you promise that you were indeed going to tell me about this."

"He insisted," said Rachel. "Jason's loyal. You know that."

"I'm not sure we're any the wiser, though, are we?" said Waverley. "All we know is that your husband was working on some secret investigation with some mystery person, and he believes the shooting links to the case."

"That's about it," said Rachel. "I'm sorry. If it helps, I was as annoyed about this as you are, but one thing I do know: Carlos was willing to put his life on the line for it, and that's good enough for me."

# Chapter 19

Rachel sat beside Carlos's bed, holding his hand. The monitors showed that he was stable. Dr Bentley had given him a hefty dose of painkiller before removing the bullet under local anaesthetic. She examined the bullet through the plastic bag in her hand, grateful to the medical and security teams for agreeing to keep the shooting secret for now.

Carlos opened his eyes.

"Welcome to the *Coral Queen* infirmary. All the best people have been here." She kissed him tenderly. He grinned.

"I think I owe you another apology for scaring you half to death."

"Later. For now, you have to stay here for a few days."

"No. I must get up. I need to meet with Helena."

She put her finger to his lips.

"Hush, darling. There's no arguing. Dr Bentley says you went into septic shock. You nearly ended up being the first patient in their ventilated bed. Your kidney function has been knocked off, so you need IV fluids. You're also on a course of IV antibiotics, so you're going nowhere. I told Waverley you were working a case, but wasn't sure how much I could say, so I didn't mention Helena by name. I said I didn't know who you were working with."

"Okay, fine. I'll stay here for a day, then I need to get back to my honeymoon."

She laughed. "You mean back to your secret world."

"That too. Thank you for covering for Helena. That must have grated. Are you still angry?"

"No. The thought of losing you helped me realise how you've felt a few times when I've got myself into scrapes. We're two of a kind, Carlos. That's why we will make a happy couple."

He relaxed his head back on the pillow. "It makes me a joyful man to hear you say that; I never wanted to hurt you. On the note of being two of a kind, Rachel, I need to ask you to let Helena know where I am. She's in room 8460; her number's on my phone under Aphrodite."

"The Greek goddess of love? I nicknamed her that too."

"It was always a joke because she has Greek heritage. She is beautiful and there were times I thought we'd make a couple, but it would never have worked. We never were, you know. I just said that because I didn't want to put you in danger by telling you what was really going on."

"At least that's something, but Aphrodite or not, that woman is not getting off lightly with almost getting you killed!"

"You're my love goddess. Remember that."

"Ah, the patient's awake." Dr Bentley joined them and checked the monitors and charts. "Where's Bernard? I thought he was looking after our renegade."

"Gone to draw up the next antibiotic dose for your restless patient," Rachel replied. "I said I'd buzz if anything happened."

"Thank you, Doctor. You saved my life, I think."

"It was touch and go, but you're not out of the woods yet. Has Rachel told you I'm keeping you in for two days?"

"I agreed to a day," Carlos answered sullenly.

"In this domain, I'm in charge. You will stay here for as long as I say you need to. Two more days, minimum. Any argument and I'll call security to keep you here, and believe me, you're not in Chief Waverley's good books."

Carlos nodded, accepting defeat. "I do feel tired. Is that the drugs or the kidneys Rachel told me about?"

"A bit of both, I should imagine. You've got what we call in the trade an acute kidney injury, but hopefully we can reverse it. You've also got a nasty infection from that bullet. Strange it should have set in so quickly. I think you should get some rest, and your wife needs to get something to eat. She's been here for hours."

Rachel was reluctant to leave, but Carlos insisted. Sarah was waiting for her in Gwen's office.

"Haven't you eaten either?" asked Rachel.

"I thought I'd wait for you. I'm off-duty now. Would you like some company?"

Rachel took her friend's arm.

"Yes please."

It was too late to eat in the premier restaurant, so they went up to the buffet. Rachel helped herself to chicken risotto while Sarah headed towards the Asian kitchen. The beauty of the buffet was there was something for every taste. And it was quiet, as most people would be in the theatre watching the late show or in other entertainment lounges and bars.

Once seated, the two women tucked in hungrily. Neither spoke while they ate; Rachel was ravenous, but soon satiated. Sarah had collected lemon squashes for them both, and Rachel sipped hers while her friend finished her curry.

"That feels better. Food is a miracle worker," said Sarah.

"I know what you mean. I didn't realise how hungry I was until I got the whiff of food; it's been quite a day. I'm sorry about dragging Jason into this, but Carlos was so insistent about coming back to the ship, I didn't know what else to do."

"Don't apologise. He was pleased you asked, and it took his mind off trying to prove my innocence. Well, pleased might not be the right word, but he was happy to be of help. You know what these ex-forces people are like. Once a soldier, always a soldier – that's why he and Carlos get on so well. He still doesn't have any idea what's going on though; says you were rather vague about it and thinks you're holding back."

"Your fiancé's right, but it involves someone else's cover and I can't blow it. Jason would understand that if he knew."

"It must have been an awful day for you. I felt bad enough about Jason's car accident; I'd be distraught if someone had shot him."

"It wasn't one of my best days, that's for sure, but we're certainly making unforgettable memories on our honeymoon. Just not quite the type I'd envisaged."

"You've got that right. At least Carlos's safe in the infirmary for a few days. I suppose you intend to seek who tried to kill your husband and find out who killed Keith? I would plead with you not to, but I'd be wasting my breath."

Rachel had been trying to figure out her next moves.

"Carlos is certain his attempted killer isn't on board the *Coral*, but I'm not sure whether he's just saying that to comfort me. I do need to speak to the person he's been meeting with, the enigmatic but ever-present Helena, and persuade her to leave him out of it from now on. Then I may well busy myself with the other investigation, you're right there. Perhaps we can work on it together?"

"Are you sure you want to do this, Rachel?"

"I might as well keep busy while Carlos is out of action. He wouldn't want me moping about."

Sarah bit her lip.

"You know something, don't you?" Rachel quizzed.

"I discovered something, but whether it has anything to do with Keith's death is another matter. While you were ashore today, I thought I'd do a little investigating of my own. I couldn't get that minister's strange behaviour out of my head. I don't like him for a start; he gives me the heebie-jeebies."

"In that case, he's guilty," laughed Rachel.

Sarah smirked. "Well, I'm not sure about that, but he's certainly up to something. Today, I sneaked into his room while he was supposed to be out on a trip."

Rachel's mouth dropped open. "You? Sarah Bradshaw sneaked into a passenger's room? What were you thinking?"

"I was thinking about Keith and how he deserves justice. I still feel guilty about the way I spoke to him the night he died, not to mention the question mark over my innocence until we find out what happened. So instead of relying on you to solve the crime, I thought it was time I took some responsibility."

Rachel frowned, but said nothing.

"Anyway, I was rifling through his safe when he came in."

*Could this day get any worse?* Rachel asked herself. Not only had her husband taken a bullet, but her best friend had been sneaking around in a potential killer's room.

She took a deep breath. "You're still here, so I take it he didn't catch you. Or did you come up with some legitimate reason for being there?"

"No, he didn't see me. I hid under the bed. You would have been so proud of me, Rachel. You're always saying nurses would make brilliant detectives."

"I didn't mean it literally, but go on."

"I heard him go out on to his balcony and was thinking of sneaking out of the suite when someone else turned up. A man."

"Who?"

"I don't know, I only saw his legs. Good calf muscles and under forty at a guess. I thought I recognised the voice though. They both went on to the balcony, but when I turned to get out, I snagged my leg on the buckle of a suitcase. It's left me with a gash."

"I noticed the dressing on your left calf."

"After that, I hit my head on the mattress and cried out. Don't worry, they didn't hear. I got out from under the bed and went to push the suitcase back in position. That's when I noticed how heavy it was, so I pulled it out. Guess what was in it?"

"If my day's anything to go by, a nuclear weapon."

"No, silly. It was cash, and lots of it. He also had a stash in his safe, but there's not enough room for the amount in that suitcase. Heaven knows why it wasn't locked."

"Perhaps he forgot to lock it, or perhaps he surmised that an unlocked suitcase would not interest the stateroom steward."

"That makes sense. So my thinking is that maybe Keith got wind of something that involved this Andrew Farmer. Having Googled him, Bernard and I discovered he's got his fingers in a lot of enormous housing projects worth billions."

"So you've dragged Bernard into this too?"

"Not really; he came into the consulting room yesterday when I was researching Farmer. He remarked on corruption and construction in his country and it got me thinking."

"Organised crime can be involved in big building projects, not to mention bribes. Corrupt politicians are always targets for criminal gangs. Politicians and police," Rachel finished in disgust.

"But why bring the money on board the ship? He made out it was a last-minute decision to take a holiday after hearing Keith talking about his planned cruise."

"That bit I don't get, unless he's doing a deal on board, but at least we have one suspect with motive. Excellent work, Sarah. But promise me you won't do anything like that again. You could lose your job, and remember, you're a pacifist. I can't bear to think what could have happened to you if he'd discovered you in his room."

Sarah looked downcast, then grinned. "I have to admit, I don't think I could take the stress again, so I can more or less promise. Give me a medical emergency any day."

"Have you told Jason about this?"

Sarah shook her head vigorously. "No way! He'd kill me. I've been wondering how to let security know about that cash, though. I was thinking an anonymous tipoff."

"You've been watching too many films, Sarah Bradshaw." The two women laughed.

"Do you think it likely Andrew Farmer is the one who killed my cousin?"

"It's difficult to imagine a strong enough motive. I would suspect that Farmer's the type to pay Keith to keep his mouth shut rather than kill him, but you just never know. He's clearly involved in some nefarious dealings that need investigating. Money laundering, bribes, who knows? Are you certain you can't remember who the man was that Farmer met with? You said you recognised the voice."

"I did, but it could have been anyone I've met over the past few days."

"Okay, I think it's time we tracked down Keith's so-called friends again to see if we can gather some clues as to motive. Any idea where they'll be at this time of night?" She looked at her watch: 11pm.

"Anywhere there's booze, I should imagine. The most popular bars are on deck five. That's a good place to start."

Rachel and Sarah wandered in and out of every bar on deck five in search of their prey. Rachel spotted the bright red hair of Jean Sutton in the Culture Lounge, where a band was playing music from the 1980s.

"There," she nodded towards the group.

"We've found them. Now what?"

"I'm not sure. Perhaps we should casually stray nearby in the hope they will call out to us. If they do, you take Max. I think he's sweet on you."

Sarah rolled her eyes. "Great!"

"Jean's a gossip, so I'll take her. See if I can get her to give up some juicy nuggets about the others that might reveal motives."

"Or eliminate them from our enquiries," laughed Sarah.

"That too."

"What about Jean? She might be the killer herself. But no, I think we could be wasting our time. Andrew Farmer's our man."

Rachel laughed. "He may well be, but the more people we eliminate, the more we can focus on your prime suspect."

Sarah giggled. "This is exciting."

"Well don't get used to it. I don't want you putting yourself at risk again. This is not a game. There's a killer on the loose who probably wouldn't think twice about terminating anyone who gets in their way." Checking Sarah's eyes to ensure her message had got through, Rachel lightened the tone. "Right, Watson, it's time."

"The right time, if you ask me. They're well-oiled."

"Exactly. That's just what we need. Plenty of drink makes for loose tongues."

# Chapter 20

The Culture Lounge was noisy with lively passengers having fun, the music booming from enormous speakers strategically placed around the whole room. The dance floor in front of the centre stage was packed with people attempting Michael Jackson's moonwalk and failing miserably, but they were enjoying themselves.

Rachel's plan worked like a dream. No sooner were they within a few feet of the boisterous friends of the late Keith Bird than they called them over.

"Nurse Sarah. Hello. Are you off-duty?" Max delivered right on cue.

Sarah feigned surprise. "Oh hello, Max. Yes, Rachel and I were just going to get ourselves a drink. I love eighties music."

*Liar*, thought Rachel, impressed that Sarah could carry the subterfuge off with such aplomb. She shouldn't have been surprised, though, as nurses probably have to be among the best actresses and actors out there, putting to one side the horrors they deal with daily so they can exude confident reassurance to the next patient.

*Similar to being in the police force*, she mused.

"Why don't you join us? Max's buying," slurred Duncan. His curly black hair reminded Rachel of a shaggy dog and made her want to pat him on the head.

"Max is always buying," Max complained. "But it would be my pleasure to buy you a drink, Sarah. And you, Rachel. Where's your new husband? Don't tell me you've tired of him already."

"Send him my way if you have," gabbled Luke.

Rachel baulked for a moment, remembering Carlos was lying downstairs in the infirmary. What was she doing leaving him so soon after an operation? Should she forget about this and head down to his bedside?

Sarah recognised her dilemma and cut in. "Carlos's meeting with family and friends this evening. Rachel's keeping me company."

Max nodded, his round eyes almost popping out of his head as he ogled Sarah. The usually quiet man was well lubricated and more chatty than usual, almost slimy this evening. Rachel shuddered.

"What can I get you ladies?"

They decided on the cocktail of the day, taking pot luck that it wouldn't be too strong. Two cosmopolitans arrived minutes later. Rachel nudged Sarah, cocking her head in the big man's direction. Sarah frowned, but complied.

Rachel smiled at Jean.

"What did you get up to today?" she asked, holding the woman's bleary green-eyed gaze. Jean's makeup remained immaculate, although the burgundy lipstick was smudging at the corners of her mouth. Her flaming red hair clung to her oval face.

"I went on a tour of Cadiz. I don't know what the others did, but I suspect it involved alcohol. Look at those two."

Rachel eyed Luke and Duncan as they moved their attention back to each other, getting closer and closer together.

"I didn't think they were an item?"

"They weren't this morning; they were arguing like a pair of alley cats. Luke's always fancied Duncan, but Duncan only had eyes for Keith. Keith kept him at arm's length, though. Strictly professional. He was heterosexual and very picky. Liked the rich and famous rather than plebs." The bitterness in her tone confirmed Rachel's suspicion that Jean had also had a thing for her boss.

"What does Duncan do again? I can't remember."

"He's the senior stylist at our Knightsbridge salon. Thinks he owns the place the way he behaves, but the customers like him, especially the gay ones. He's had a few flings with clients, I can tell you."

Rachel noted the use of 'our' salon, but parked it.

"Really? Anyone famous I might know?"

"One's an MP, high up in government, but the guy's married, so I'd better not say who. It might land him in the headlines."

Rachel's interest piqued, but she didn't think such a revelation would make headlines these days, unless the MP was also Prime Minister.

"What about Luke? How do you know him?"

"He's an old friend of Keith's. They went to business school together. He's not got much of a head for business though; has a string of failed start-ups behind him. Most of them funded by his cousin, Max."

"I didn't realise he and Max were cousins." Sarah had told her this when she had introduced them at the captain's cocktail party, but Rachel reckoned Jean had been too fixated on Carlos at the time to have been listening. She was right.

"Why would you? They don't get on that well, anyway."

"So does Luke have a business at present?"

"He has a salon, but he won't have it for much longer. We're opening a sister salon in direct competition. Keith was ruthless like that, but Luke would have failed anyway. He doesn't have a head for business."

Rachel's ears pricked up. "What did Luke think about that?"

"He didn't know, but I told him about it on the first night of the cruise. We were trading insults and it slipped out. He was livid. Said he would have it out with Keith during the cruise."

"And do you know if he had it out with him?"

"I'm not sure. Things were pretty tense on that first night." Jean suddenly realised what she was implying and put her hand to her mouth.

Rachel pretended not to notice. "Keith could be a handful. Shame he didn't think about going into partnership with Luke."

Jean spluttered a laugh. "Keith and Luke? No way Keith would ever have gone into business with him."

"But why would he go into direct competition with Luke if he was his friend?" asked Rachel.

"Friendship came second with Keith. It was always about the money. That's what interested him, nothing else. Women, friends, they were second."

Rachel nodded thoughtfully. Keith was worse than she'd imagined. Jean took a huge slurp of the cocktail she held. The straw almost collapsed under the strain.

"I expect Keith confided in you, though."

Jean's huge lips pouted. "I was his confidante. He did nothing without talking to me first."

Rachel very much doubted this was the case, considering the woman's penchant for gossip, but she nodded sympathetically.

"It must have been quite a shock, losing him like that. What will happen to the business now?"

"I don't know what will happen to the business. And for your information, yes, it was a shock. That nurse friend of yours was the last to see him. They argued. I heard her threaten him."

Jean tried to stand up straight to show how she meant business, but ended up in a crumpled mess. She flopped back on to the bench seat. Rachel sat next to her.

"Do you know of anyone else who might have had it in for your friend?" she asked gently.

"Apart from her, you mean?" Jean bored holes through Sarah's head while she was busy speaking with Max, oblivious. Everything was going to plan.

"Sarah wouldn't have killed her cousin. I've known her since we were kids. She couldn't harm anyone."

"Humph. If you say so."

"So could anyone else have had it in for him? You seem like someone who knew him extremely well. I expect he depended on you and, as you say, shared everything with you."

"Yes, he did. He wasn't popular with everyone, mind. There are a few in this group who would have liked to see the back of him."

"Why do you say that?"

"Did I tell you Luke had it in for him for opening that rival salon?" Jean's speech was becoming more slurred and she was getting louder. No-one appeared to notice, apart from Sarah, who raised her eyebrows.

"I think you mentioned that, yes."

"Then there was Max."

"I thought he was just an investor. Surely the salon was making enough money to give him a good return?" This was new to Rachel. It had crossed her mind that Max could be involved, but when she discovered how rich he was, she thought it unlikely.

"Two things there. One, Keith didn't like to be in anyone's debt. He liked to be in full control. He hadn't told Max about the second salon and was going to open it on the quiet with profit from our first salon. Come to think of it, that might have been why Keith was so angry when he found out I'd told Luke about it." Jean waved her arm at the waiter, pointing at her glass to indicate she was ready for another. Rachel didn't think she would be coherent for too much longer, so dug a little deeper.

"And the other reason?"

"What reason? Sorry, I lost my thread there. What were we talking about? I like you, Raquel. You're easy to talk to."

Deciding not to correct her on the name, Rachel persevered.

"You were saying there were a couple of reasons Max might have been angry with Keith."

"Was I? Oh dear, I can't remember. I think I might dance now. Come on, you guys, stop smooching and dance."

"We're not smooching, lovey. Man talk."

Jean gave them a look of disdain as she took the next drink from the waiter.

"I need the little girls' room." She pushed herself up from the bench and staggered towards the exit to find the nearest toilet.

"I'll go and check on her. She might need some help," said Duncan. "She can't hold her drink."

"Or her tongue. I wouldn't listen to anything she says, lovey; most of it's pure fiction," grunted Luke, clearly disappointed at the departure of his friend. It was obvious he couldn't care less about Jean's state.

Max didn't seem to have noticed Jean and Duncan's disappearance and was still commandeering Sarah's attention. Rachel considered trying Luke, but he slumped back in his chair in a huff, staring out at the dance floor.

Sarah signalled a help sign.

"Come on, Sarah, time to go. Didn't you say you were meeting Jason at half past midnight?"

"Oh yes, I did. Good talking to you, Max. Enjoy the rest of your cruise."

Taking Rachel's arm, Sarah walked with her towards the exit.

"Thank you so much. He was getting creepy. He's bad enough sober, but spine-chillingly slimy when drunk."

They passed Jean coming out of the ladies.

"Where's Duncan?" Rachel asked.

"How should I know? Probably gone to chat someone else up, or he's had enough of Luke's whining." The woman staggered and stopped herself falling by leaning her hand on the wall. "You know what? I think it's time I went to bed. You wouldn't see me to my room, would you, Raquel?"

"Raquel?" Sarah mouthed.

Rachel grinned. "We'll both see you back. What floor?"

Jean handed Rachel the room card. Sarah looked over her shoulder.

"She's on the eighth."

"I'm not sure I should get in the lift with a murderer, but as long as Raquel's here, you can come along."

"Why, thank you," said Sarah, following behind, hands on hips. "And I'm not a murderer."

"If you say so, love. Raquel, can I take your arm? I don't feel all that steady."

"Of course." Rachel pulled Sarah from behind to take the woman's other arm, but Sarah had gone indignant, and Jean was leaning more and more heavily on Rachel. Any minute now, she would be carrying her.

"Sarah, could you help?" She spoke through gritted teeth.

"Okay, but as a murderer, I might just let her go."

Rachel chuckled, but Sarah did her bit and they got Jean to her room. Sarah took the card and unlocked the door.

"You should be careful who you give your card to," she said. Jean almost fell and they had to assist her inside.

"I think you should get straight to bed," Rachel said.

"I feel—" Sarah dodged and Jean puked all over Rachel's shorts. Rachel glared at Sarah.

"You could have warned me."

Sarah laughed. "Your friend, your puke."

They helped Jean into the bathroom, where she brought up the rest of the alcohol she'd imbibed. Leaning her head over the toilet bowl, Jean mumbled a few words.

"Reminds me of college."

"Yeah, me too. Not," said Sarah caustically.

"Give me a break, love. Your friend said you weren't a murderer and I believe her. You could be nicer, though. Aren't you supposed to be a nurse?"

Sarah put her hand to her mouth, mortified. She was never usually rude to passengers. Rachel wondered again what was eating at her friend. Something had happened to Sarah since she went back to the UK. Rachel needed to find out what it was, but for the moment, her greater need was to wash her shorts.

"Do you mind if I use your sink to wipe these down?"

"Raquel, you can use anything you like. Use the bin bag in the pedal, I haven't put anything in there. I'm sure Nurse Death here can find you a pair of shorts in one of my drawers."

Sarah pulled a face behind Jean's back that reminded Rachel of when they were kids. She stifled a giggle.

"I'll help," Sarah said, closing the door of the bathroom before both of them doubled up laughing.

# Chapter 21

S arah marched indignantly back towards the lift.

"I really don't like that woman. She knows how to wind people up. I bet Keith didn't like her either."

"Hang on, Sarah, we have another stop." Rachel showed her the key card wallet in her hand. Sarah's mouth dropped open before she shook her head.

"No way, I've done enough sneaking around for one day. Where did you get that anyway? Why didn't you tell me about it before?"

"It was in a drawer in Jean's room, along with this." Rachel pulled a document wallet from behind her back.

"How come I didn't see them?"

"You were on a guilt trip and went to check on our sick patient. While you were gone, I thought I might as well have a little poke around, and voila!" She held both items in the air before tucking the wallet back inside the waistband of Jean's shorts, where it nestled against her back under the t-shirt.

Sarah paused, but refrained from the rebuke she had seemed about to give her.

"I wasn't on a guilt trip. I'm a nurse, remember?"

"Something *you'd* do well to remember next time she calls you Nurse Death."

Sarah laughed and then hesitated for a moment before nodding.

"Come on, then. Let's get on with it."

They did an about-turn and headed down to the other end of the corridor. There was no tape outside the room, as Waverley wouldn't want to draw passengers' attention to it. Rachel slipped the key card into the slot and heard the lock click open, pleased the code hadn't been changed. That was the first thing she would have done in Waverley's shoes, but obviously he hadn't felt the need.

She turned the lights on by inserting the card. Unsurprisingly, Keith had taken a luxury suite at the end of the corridor. It was identical to the one she and Carlos were in, courtesy of Marjorie. His bags were packed, ready for removal to the purser's office; otherwise, the room was made up ready for the next unsuspecting guest.

"I thought they might have moved these already. Good for us, though."

"Not a priority," said Sarah. "The room's paid for, so why block up the purser's office? They'll most likely be moved out the night before disembarkation, ready for his next of kin. My poor aunt. She'll be distraught. He was probably not all she and my uncle wanted in a son, but he was still their son."

Rachel nodded. "You're right; sorry, Sarah. I shouldn't have brought you here, it was thoughtless. Would you like me to do this alone?"

Tears filled Sarah's eyes just as the door opened. Jason stood in the doorway and Sarah ran to him, crying. His straight face softened as he held her.

"How did you know we were here?" asked Rachel.

"I've had one member of the team watching this room permanently. You're lucky I was the one watching the screen tonight. You won't find anything. I've checked and double checked. I think someone got in here before we did."

"But don't you save footage?" asked Rachel.

"It had been taped over by the time I went to check it. Who had the key?"

"I found it in Jean Sutton's room. Don't look at me like that, Jason. She was drunk and we helped her back to her room."

Sarah recovered from her tears and laughed. "Then she was sick down Rachel's shorts. It was so funny, Jason. Except the part where she kept repeating that I was a murderer and called me Nurse Death."

Jason lifted Sarah's chin up. "The prettiest Nurse Death I've ever seen." He smirked as he kissed her forehead.

"And she kept calling Rachel 'Raquel'. That was the funniest."

Jason smiled at them both, but focussed on Rachel. "So why do you think she had a key? I had checked and we issued two, but there was no record of who had the other one. His friends denied knowing there was another key."

"Maybe they were seeing each other. She certainly had the hots for him. Or perhaps they were going to do some business. She is his accountant."

"Then why deny having a key?"

"People get silly with murder. They think we arrest people willy-nilly. I guess she was just plain scared."

"You don't think it's her, then?" asked Jason. "She was the last person to see him after Sarah left, because I don't believe for one moment she went back to her room."

"I can't see it being her. She's ambitious and had designs on going into partnership with him, probably through marriage."

"That would not happen. Not according to Duncan. He said Keith had decided to sack her for opening her big gob, as he put it, about a second salon he'd been keeping under wraps."

"Mm, maybe Carlos was right."

"Right about what?" asked Sarah.

"He reminded me of the woman spurned adage, but I still don't believe it's her. I just don't."

"Why?" asked Jason.

"My gut."

"Oh no, not that again, Rachel. Don't say that to Waverley," laughed Sarah.

"Did you find anything else out? I take it you didn't just happen upon Miss Sutton in the corridor?"

"Maybe not. We scouted the bars to track down Keith's friends. So guilty as charged. Does Jean have responsibility for his belongings?" Rachel felt the document folder digging into her back.

"No. His belongings will be handed over to his parents when we reach Southampton. They want to collect them and meet with the chief. I just hope we've found out who did it by then."

"All I discovered from Jean, who's a colander when it comes to leaking information, was that Luke was furious about Keith's plan to move in on his patch. Luke apparently doesn't make excellent business decisions. Duncan had a crush on Keith, but his interest wasn't exclusive. He had affairs with clients. One was an MP."

"Andrew Farmer!" exclaimed Sarah. "I told you, Rachel. He's our man."

"What's this?" asked Jason.

Rachel did a Waverley cough to warn Sarah off saying any more.

"Sarah feels that Andrew Farmer is corrupt and, as a client of Keith's, may have been compromised in some way. She Googled him."

Jason raised an eyebrow, but smiled tenderly at Sarah.

"Bernard agrees with me."

"See what I'm dealing with?" laughed Rachel. "Jean was going to tell me something about Max, but the drink took over and she lost the plot. We rescued her outside the ladies and helped her up to her room."

"Raquel helped her, Nurse Death tried to trip her up."

Jason laughed so hard his hand flew up to his sore neck.

"Oh darling, I'm sorry. Are you still in pain? Where's your collar?"

Rachel watched the tender scene. They were made for each other. She wondered why they hadn't set a date for the wedding and realised that might be why her friend was so unlike herself at the moment.

"What about you? Did you find anything out from Max? Jason, I have to warn you, you have a rival for Sarah's affections."

"Yeah, I saw him drooling over her in the Culture Lounge."

"Why didn't you tell us you already saw us there?" asked Sarah.

"Just checking you would be truthful. It wouldn't be the first time PC – sorry, DS Prince has kept us mere security guards out of the loop."

Rachel's hand reached to the document folder, digging in her back, with a tinge of guilt. Sarah punched him on the arm.

"You're unbearable tonight. What is it with you?"

Jason held Sarah's face in his hands and stared lovingly into her eyes.

"I've been trying to track you down. We haven't spoken much since we set sail, and then with all the events of the past few days, I couldn't find the right time. Then I decided there would never be a perfect time. Forgive me, Rachel, I have to say this."

"Don't mind me, I'm enjoying it."

He turned his face back towards Sarah. "That car accident made me think. I don't want to leave this world without being your husband. Let's set the date."

Sarah sighed heavily. "Not unless—"

"I know. I've already written to my parents and posted the letter today. When we're next on shore leave, we'll visit them together and invite them to the wedding. I realise resistance is futile. I love you, Sarah Bradshaw, with all my heart."

*So that little puzzle is solved*, thought Rachel.

"You know what? I think I'll leave you two alone," she said, happy for Sarah and keen to discover the contents of the document folder nudging against her back.

\*\*\*

Sarah called Rachel as soon as she got back to her room. Jason was working the rest of the night and she wanted to explain why she'd been so crabby.

"Did I wake you?"

"No, I've just taken a shower and changed. I'm going down to spend some time with Carlos. I need to talk to him anyway."

"Bernard's manning the infirmary. He'll let you have a bed so you can get some sleep. I'll call him when we're finished, but thought I'd better tell you why I've been so snappy lately."

"I think I got the gist, but go ahead. Something to do with Jason's family?"

"Jason had a horrible upbringing. His parents drank and argued the whole time he was growing up. His sister's followed in their footsteps, as far as I can gather."

"Is that why he's teetotal?"

"Yes. He said that drink ruined his childhood and his parents' marriage. He left home at fourteen, went to stay with his uncle, who he dotes on. His uncle never married, but still took Jason in as though he were his own. They have a real father/son bond. Before he left home, Jason used to stay over when it all got too much for him. He says he tried to get his sister to go too, but she was older and out with her friends most of the time.

"One day, he was trying to study for a maths test and the shouting started. He flipped. Went downstairs, told them he was leaving and not coming back."

"Did they try to stop him?"

"No. They were too drunk. He turned up at his uncle's house and told him he'd left home. That was it. He never went back. Soon afterwards, his parents lost their jobs because of their drinking and moved out of area. Rachel, he's not seen them since."

"And you want them at your wedding because—?"

"Because he's still tormented by those memories. His uncle Sid tells him they don't drink anymore, and both are in poor health because of past abuse. I feel he needs to see them, or he'll regret it if they die and he hasn't tried. He's always refused. I got angry and talked about forgiveness. We had row after row, until about six weeks ago, I told him I would not marry him unless he invited them."

"And that went down well, I'm sure."

"Oh yeah. Really well. I've never seen him so upset. All the rejection he'd felt throughout his young life came back and hit him hard. I tried to explain that it was himself he was punishing, damaging even, for as long as he held on to this sore, it would fester and stop him from being a man."

"Wow! That's quite a statement, Sarah. I'm not sure I'd have had the guts."

"He has to try to make peace with them, Rachel. I don't care whether or not they come to the wedding, although as you know, I'm a sucker for happy endings. But if he doesn't invite them, it wouldn't feel right. I'm resigned to his rejection issues from his fiancée breaking up with him, but this goes deeper."

"I'm happy for you he's come around, if only so that I can have the nice Sarah back."

Sarah laughed as she put the phone down. She was so happy she could burst, and hoped against hope that she was doing the right thing. Now she couldn't sleep because she was feeling so excited.

She rang down to the infirmary; Bernard picked up.

"How's the patient?"

"He's awake. He has a visitor. A woman."

"Don't tell me – a Greek goddess kind of woman?"

"She's Italian, but yes, she has lovely hair."

"What does she want?"

"I don't know. Carlos insisted I let her in after he called her. They're speaking Italian, so I can't make anything out. It sounds serious though. Does she have anything to do with what happened to Rachel and Carlos in Cadiz?"

Sarah's heart sank as she blew out a heavy breath. "I suspect she might have, but Rachel's being cagey. Bernard, you need to tell them that Rachel is on her way down and she won't be happy to find Aphrodite there."

"Her name's Helena—" He giggled. "Oh, I see, the goddess of love. Okay. Hang on a minute, I'll let them know—"

Sarah waited until Bernard picked up the phone again.

"She's leaving. Anything else I can do for you, ma'am?" he chided.

"Would you let Rachel sleep down there? I'll come down early and make up a new bed."

"No problem, but you don't need to do that. You sound chirpy tonight. I guess you and Jason have made up."

"I don't know how you would know about that, but yes, I am happy. Jason and I are setting a date."

"At last! Which one of you conceded about whatever it was bothering the two of you?"

"Him, of course," she chuckled.

"Us men always have to give in. You women do not understand how much we suffer."

"Don't let Brigitte hear you say that, or she'll give you a lecture on the frailties of men."

"She already did earlier. Nothing was right. Men this and men that. Why can't we understand how irritating we are, blah, blah."

Sarah laughed. Bernard always got the sharp end of Brigitte's tongue if she had argued with her boyfriend. Brigitte was strong-willed, but she had met her match in Novak.

"Poor Bernard, and now you're outnumbered since our new doctor is also a woman."

"I would gladly be surrounded by a room full of women if you promised me our new doctor would not be one of them. Although I don't think we need to worry on that front; I think Graham will have her moved soon. He's had enough of how she speaks to people already. She's terrorising the crew, who are now too frightened to get sick. She told Brian he was a malingerer. I spent my break in the crew bar, consoling her latest victims before coming to the infirmary again."

"That's what you say. Are you sure it wasn't so you could sell some of your stingers?"

"I promise I was not. I was there as a counsellor. They are traumatised, Sarah."

The junior doctor on board the cruise ship was responsible for the health of the crew while the chief, Graham, was mainly responsible for passengers and officers. They intermingled when on call, but that was the general rule. Brillo had only been on board for four days and she was already creating havoc.

"Graham won't like her upsetting the crew one little bit."

"Nope, she'll be getting her cards. If she doesn't, we can club together to ask for a transfer. Mutiny's always an option."

"Don't even joke about such things. Goodnight, Bernard. I'll see you in the morning."

# Chapter 22

Rachel didn't get the opportunity to discuss what she'd found in Keith's document wallet with Carlos because he seemed drained after updating her on the Helena situation. Instead, she spent the night in the infirmary and left him still sleeping. Bernard assured her he was stable and encouraged her to go for a run.

Running helped blow the cobwebs from her brain. She had forgotten to let Helena know where Carlos was and couldn't work out whether that was a deliberate omission. She was miffed when Carlos told her he had called Helena anyway, but pleased to hear that the man who'd shot him had been tracked down. Helena had asked an old spy pal to keep an eye on Carlos and Rachel in Cadiz. When he saw Carlos fall, he scanned the area with binoculars and saw a man leaving with what appeared to be a fishing rod bag. The bag contained the rifle, and through his connections, the ex-spy had been able to have the man arrested for carrying an unlicensed weapon.

"Is that all?" she asked.

"They couldn't admit to him having shot me, could they? It's enough for now."

Rachel ran round and round deck sixteen. There was no longer any reason to avoid Helena, and she needed to talk to her about the contents of Keith's documents. Whether they were linked to Keith's death was questionable.

She had never liked Keith, but now it was obvious that not many people did. She was not surprised about his ambition, but did think that moving in on his so-called friend's patch was a low move, even for him. Luke didn't strike her as a killer, but that didn't mean he wasn't. He clearly had a dogged determination to succeed, despite numerous failed business attempts if Jean Sutton was to be believed.

Jean herself was a conundrum. One minute she was gushing about Keith and the next she was derogatory. Was it just a woman spurned thing, or could there be more to it?

Max was a quandary. Why did he invest so much money in Keith's business? Had he found out about the new salon? Even if he had, it was a poor motive for murder. Her suspicion was that Keith might have had something on Max – she wouldn't put it past him to use it to extort money. It was odd that Max continued to fund the dysfunctional group's excesses in the way he did since Keith's death, though.

*Maybe he is just inadequate and feels he has to buy friends, or perhaps, as Carlos suggested, he has so much money, it's small change to him.*

The only one who didn't appear to have any real motive was Duncan, but she wasn't ready to rule him out yet. He was apparently well able to take care of business while also taking full advantage of the salon's clientele. Could there be something in his relationships that he wanted to hide? If the MP he'd had an affair with turned out to be Andrew Farmer, that would make him a definite person of interest.

Realising she'd been running for forty minutes, Rachel decided to head to the buffet for breakfast. Then she could change and shower before visiting Carlos.

The ship was docked in Malaga. She sighed; she and Carlos had been due to go on a trip for the day to get away from the busy port. She arrived at the buffet and collected a bowl of fruit and a pastry.

The hustle and bustle of the buffet always cheered her. Happy passengers nattered over breakfast with family and newfound friends, no doubt getting ready for the day ashore. It was going to be another scorcher. The temperature had been rising during her run.

Rachel was finishing her third mug of coffee when a familiar figure stopped by her table.

"May I join you?"

Rachel shrugged her shoulders. "I don't own the table."

*Why does this woman bring out the stroppy teenager in me?*

Helena flashed a disarming smile as she placed a tray of food on the table.

"I don't blame you for being annoyed with me. If I were in your position, I'd feel the same."

Rachel didn't trust herself to answer, so she put her mug out for another coffee when a waiter appeared at the table.

"And for you, ma'am?" he asked Helena.

"Decaf, please."

After the waiter left them to their drinks, Helena persisted in speaking to Rachel as if she were a friend. Rachel couldn't help but admire the woman's audacity. If nothing else, she was able to give the impression to those around that she and Rachel were long-lost buddies.

Helena was older than Rachel, but extremely attractive. The big brown eyes were focussed, but the dullness behind the happy exterior suggested she was world worn. Rachel softened.

"Carlos never got the opportunity to tell me what you asked him to get involved with."

"I am sorry about Carlos getting hurt. I tried to prevent it. Someone must have seen me talking to him. My cover is blown, to some extent. Carlos told me you covered for me with security – thank you."

"How do you know you're not being watched now?"

"Once I knew I was being followed, it was easy to find the lackey on my tail. I planted some stolen jewellery in his room last night. He was arrested after dinner." Helena smiled wearily.

"So what is it you've involved my husband in?"

Helena checked the immediate vicinity to ensure they weren't being overheard. "It's a matter of national security to both your country and mine, but as Carlos trusts you, I can tell you this. There has been a lot of money moving between the two countries. We believe a rogue Mafia cell is operating in London and plans to disrupt our government using terrorist acts. The trouble is these people have tentacles everywhere and there's a leak within the Italian security agency. I am more or less alone in this, but have some old contacts I can trust."

"Like Carlos." Rachel smiled wryly. "But if you were the one being followed, why did they attack Carlos and not you?"

"That I don't know. I suspect they want me isolated so they can continue their work. Perhaps they couldn't risk killing me, knowing my boss would send a team after them."

"So you know who they are?"

"Getting there. I report to my boss via a burner phone, so we're not traced. I have two suspects, but not enough evidence to nail them so far."

"And they are?"

"I'm sorry, I can't tell you. I just wanted you to know why Carlos agreed to help, that's all."

"Thanks for what you have said, at least. Now, perhaps I can help you."

Helena's eyes brightened as the corners of her eyes creased. She leaned forward, but then grinned.

"I know. Keep Carlos out of it. Don't worry, I don't want him to get hurt, although if it's any consolation, the shooting was a warning rather than an assassination. Assassins don't miss. Can I see the bullet? The nurse told Carlos you had it."

Rachel reached into her handbag, once again annoyed this woman had Carlos's ear, and brought out the plastic bag, being careful not to let anyone else see it.

"I guess I can be grateful it wasn't a kill shot."

Helena studied the bullet for a few minutes.

"It's a dirty bullet. I wondered how the wound had caused sepsis so soon. It's been deliberately contaminated with bacteria."

"How do you know that?"

"It's the discolouration and the way the bullet has loose shards. That's deliberate, almost like an injection of poison. We know there are underground labs experimenting with this kind of thing. Would you be happy for me to send it away for analysis?"

Rachel thought for a few moments before nodding.

"I really can help you with your case. I found this last night." She pushed the wallet she'd been intending to show to Carlos across the table. Helena opened the document case and read the contents, intensity and focus deepening as she pored over them.

"I assume that one man you suspect of being involved is the government minister, Andrew Farmer?"

Helena raised her head. "Carlos said you were good. He's right. Where did you get these?"

"It's a long story, but I'm investigating the murder of an old acquaintance. He's the cousin of my best friend."

"Carlos mentioned that."

Rachel felt irritation growing again. Her husband appeared to tell this woman far more about her than she had realised.

"Anyway, the man who was murdered, Keith Bird, ran a high-class hairdressing salon in London. I believe that he picked up information about various clients and may have hoped to make money from it. In this case, he obviously found these documents and held on to them. But I think he'd bitten off more than he bargained for and didn't know what to do about it. He was on the run, even applied for a job on board this ship."

"But all these documents show is that Farmer signed off on some large construction deals. It's not enough to incriminate him."

"He has a stash of cash under the bed in his room. I believe he's going to make a deal on board this ship. You should be able to catch him in the act, especially if you involve the chief of security, Jack Waverley, and Jason Goodridge, my friend's fiancé. I can vouch for both. They are honest and incorruptible, and could help you with your spy stuff. Who's the other man you suspect is involved?"

Helena swallowed just enough to hint that she knew more than she was going to let on.

"I'm sorry, I really can't tell you. Do you think the murder you're investigating is linked to my investigation?"

"I didn't think so last night, but who knows? Sarah, my friend, is convinced Andrew Farmer killed Keith."

"No. I don't believe that's right, it's not his MO. Farmer's only interested in money and bribes. I suspect someone's pulling his strings, it doesn't seem likely that he could be the ringleader. I need to think about this before speaking to anyone. I'm not in a great position with regards to trust right now, but perhaps you and I could work together on this."

"I'm not sure."

"Think about it. If the two cases are linked, by helping me, you'll help find the person who killed your friend."

"He wasn't my friend."

"Then why bother?"

"Because my best friend, his cousin, was seen arguing with him on the night he was killed, which puts her in the frame. I know she didn't do it, so I have to find out who did. His friends are high on my list of suspects. Farmer was on Sarah's, and another woman Keith knew might know something."

"You didn't tell me where you got these documents."

"And you didn't tell me the significance of the names Keith circled in them." Keith had circled two names. Rachel was certain they must have caught the other woman's attention.

"Touché."

Rachel picked up the documents. "If you want to work with me, you need to level with me, and so far, you've done nothing to gain my trust or cooperation other than getting my husband shot."

Rachel left the buffet, feeling that at least for the moment, she had the upper hand.

# Chapter 23

Carlos insisted Rachel take the tour of Malaga with Sarah once he discovered Sarah had a day off. It didn't take much persuasion, as Rachel felt the need to get off the ship after her conversation with Helena.

"Are you sure you don't mind? I feel terrible leaving you."

"Rachel, you were here all night. Anyway, I'm feeling much better, and if I get a good day's rest, you never know – Dr Bentley might let me out of here."

Carlos still looked pale, and now Helena had mentioned the dirty bullet theory, it made sense why he had gone downhill so quickly. He was usually so fit. It had bothered her that he'd passed out on the beach and developed sepsis within the space of a few hours.

She shared Helena's dirty bullet theory with him.

"That explains a lot. I thought maybe I was becoming soft."

"You'll get over this, Carlos."

"What do you think of Helena now you've had a chance to meet?" he asked.

"She's dedicated, focussed and secretive. There's also a sadness about her; I guess it comes from so many years of living in the shadows. Not your type at all now I've spoken to her."

"She wasn't always that way, but as you say, being a spy takes its toll. She's brilliant at what she does, and I admire her courage and determination."

"I don't doubt it, but she's older than her years."

"I didn't tell you this, but her fiancé was killed in a car accident. Helena never mentions him. It's as if he didn't exist. Since then she has given everything to her country, one hundred and ten percent."

Rachel felt a sudden compassion for the woman she had been wary of. "That's so sad. I don't know what I'd do if anything like that happened to you. Yesterday was almost too much to bear."

"All the more reason to take advantage of what we have. Now it's time for you to get out for the day and have some fun. I'm safe here and not going anywhere. Chief Waverley and Jason are coming at ten to interview me."

"Wouldn't you like some moral support?"

"No, I'll be fine. I'll tell them everything, but I won't identify Helena. That will be my one condition."

"I did suggest to her that she involve them. Try to get her to trust them when you see her."

"Okay, deal. Oh dear, look who's coming."

Brillo Sin breezed into the infirmary and picked up Carlos's chart without a word to either of them. Brigitte was behind her in an instant.

"Is there anything I can do for you, Doctor?"

Rachel sensed the tension rise between the two women. Sarah had given her enough lowdown on the new doctor to make her aware that things weren't going smoothly.

Ignoring Brigitte, Brillo marched around to the side of Carlos's bed and took his right arm.

"How's the shoulder this morning?"

"Much better, thank you, Doctor." Carlos produced one of his most endearing smiles.

"Your kidney function is improving. What I don't understand is why you ignored this abscess. Sepsis is extremely serious, you know."

"I'm sorry, Doctor, but I was on honeymoon. I'm sure you understand I didn't want to ruin things for my wife."

Brillo cracked a hint of a grin. "Yes, well, I suppose. Anyway, if things continue the way they are and our nurses don't make any mistakes, you'll be out of here tomorrow."

Brigitte opened her mouth to retort, but Sarah had appeared just in time to overhear the last part of the conversation and shook her head at her. Brillo replaced the chart at the end of the bed and left the infirmary without another word.

"I swear, I won't be held responsible for my actions if that woman continues as she is. And why doesn't she do something with that hair?"

The other three burst out laughing and Brigitte eventually joined in.

"At least you managed to get an almost smile out of her, my darling," said Rachel.

"I thought you were exaggerating when you told me about her, but that's a woman I wouldn't want to cross," replied Carlos. "Where's Dr Bentley?"

"Relax. He'll be in later. Brillo's got the day off now, so hopefully you won't have to see her again," said Sarah.

Carlos leaned back against his pillows. "That's good. Have a great day out, you two. Brigitte will take care of me."

Rachel kissed him tenderly on the lips and Sarah almost had to pull her away before she changed her mind.

"Don't worry, I've got this," reassured Brigitte. "I'll make sure he gets plenty of rest and feed him up, so that when you get back, he'll be brimming with energy."

Rachel was quiet on the way off the ship. At least she knew her husband was in good hands and couldn't come to any harm in the infirmary. Even the idea of Helena visiting him no longer filled her with dread.

In spite of herself, she had found she almost liked the woman when they spoke over breakfast. In many ways, they were similar in terms of dedication to duty and a desire to fight for justice. They were both loyal and determined to protect the public and their countries from harm.

She wondered what it would be like to be a spy. It was hard to imagine that Carlos had lived that kind of double life before she knew him. There were still some things in his past he didn't speak about, particularly his time in the SAS. She knew he was haunted by something that happened during a tour of Afghanistan, when he'd lost a friend, and now she realised there were likely other memories that he couldn't or wouldn't talk about. She empathised with Sarah because Jason had issues relating to his time in service. If their marriage was to work, Rachel needed to come to terms with the latest revelations about her husband's past, and she determined to do so.

"You're miles away, Rachel Prince. Our coach is there." Sarah's voice broke through the thoughts that threatened to overwhelm her.

"Sorry. It's hard to accept that the man you've married used to be a spy."

Sarah took her arm. "There are worse things he could have been."

"Such as?"

"Oh, I don't know… a cigarette manufacturer?"

Rachel laughed. "Where did that come from?"

"Not sure. I guess, somewhere in my subconscious, I wish tobacco had never been discovered. It causes far too much illness and death."

"On that cheerful note, I will try to be happy that my husband didn't make money from tobacco."

They boarded the bus that would be taking them to Caminito del Rey, where they would enjoy a hike along the suspended footpath renowned for having spectacular views due to its height and position within a gorge.

"Hey, you two, come and join us."

Rachel swallowed hard on hearing the squeaky voice of Jean Sutton. She was sitting at the back of the coach with Max, and patted to two seats beside them.

Sarah muttered, "That's all I need. A morning out with Max."

Max was next to the window, taking up two of the five back row seats. Rachel was happy to join them to see if she could glean any further information.

"Come on," she whispered to Sarah, "we might find out something else about Keith."

Her friend's face brightened at the prospect.

"Okay, but I'm taking the window seat furthest away from him."

Rachel grinned at Jean as she sat down. "How are you feeling this morning?"

"I've got a really bad head. To be honest, I don't remember much about last night. I was talking to you in the Culture Lounge, but from there on in, it's a blank."

"Sarah and I saw you back to your room. You were sick."

"I gathered that from the state of the bathroom. Thanks for doing that. I don't usually get drunk. It must have been the cocktails the boys plied me with."

"Where are Duncan and Luke?"

"Not sure. They were going to join us, but perhaps they had too much to drink as well. Did they say anything to you, Max?"

"Nah. Duncan left when you did last night. Luke sulked around for a while, then said he was going to join an LGBT group for drinks. It was something listed in the *Coral News*. I stayed and had a few drinks, then headed to bed. I did try calling Duncan this morning, but he didn't pick up. I guess he was still asleep. Hello, Sarah," he called, leaning forward to peer round Rachel. Sarah just grunted a response and continued looking out of the window.

"She's a bit tired today," Rachel explained. "Had a late night with her fiancé." She hoped to deflect Max's unwelcome attention from her friend by mentioning Jason. "He's a security guard on board."

"Oh. That must be an interesting job. No wonder she's not been arrested yet," sniped Jean.

Not the opening Rachel wanted, but she'd take it. "Who do you think would have wanted to kill Keith? It certainly wasn't Sarah who, by the way, cleaned you up last night after you were sick everywhere, including down my shorts." Sarah glanced Rachel's way and smiled gratefully before continuing her study of the world outside the coach. "You lent me a pair of yours. I'll get them laundered and returned later."

Max stroked his hefty chin. "I've been wondering about that myself. The killer, I mean. Didn't you see anyone else that night, Jean?"

"No. I told you, and that chief of security who keeps coming around asking questions, I left him and that nurse arguing. I didn't see anyone else. Although I did see you heading that way, Max, when I was going back downstairs, now I think of it. How did I forget that? I'd had a few drinks myself."

Sarah stiffened next to Rachel, and all three women looked at Max, waiting for an explanation.

"I don't remember seeing you. I did try to find Keith that night; he had been drinking heavily and something spooked him in the Cigar Lounge. I wanted to check he was all right, but I never found him."

"You never said anything before about trying to find him, or about something happening in the Cigar Lounge." Jean's eyes narrowed as she stared at the man sitting next to her.

"I've only just remembered about the lounge, and as for looking for him, I didn't find him so there was nothing to say. Surely you can't think I would have killed him? We were business partners."

"But you argued the night before the wedding and the cruise, didn't you? Now I remember – we'd gone to the pub. You left early. Keith said he needed to talk to you about something. He said he was going to have it out with you."

"I don't know what you're talking about." Beads of sweat appeared on Max's forehead. "We didn't argue. Keith was my friend. It was you he'd had enough of. You and your gossip. Duncan told me Keith was ready to fire you. His exact words were: 'No amount of tax saving is worth the cost of her big gob.' So there."

Jean was rendered speechless; she folded her arms across her chest and huffed.

"What was it that spooked Keith in the Cigar Lounge?" Rachel asked.

"I don't know. One minute he was talking away, the next he stubbed out a half-smoked cigar and said he'd see me later. He must have seen someone he didn't want to see. He's been twitchy recently, scared of his own shadow. No-one else noticed, but I did. Now I remember something else. He did tell me that he wanted to talk to you in your professional capacity as a police officer, Rachel."

Now it was Jean's turn to stiffen. "You never said you were police."

"There was no reason to. I have no authority on a cruise ship, and if you remember, I'm on honeymoon."

"You knew Keith was someone's target, didn't you?" Jean stared accusingly at Rachel. Sarah intervened.

"You're letting your imagination get away with you. Rachel hadn't seen my cousin in years. He gate crashed her

231

wedding, along with you lot. In fact, that's what I was arguing with him about on the night you say you saw me."

The coach drew to a halt at their destination. Jean was up out of her seat before anyone else.

"Well if you think I'm going to walk along one of the most dangerous walkways in the world with Nurse Death and a cop who, for all we know, could be trying to set us up for the murder of our friend, you can think again. Max, are you coming?"

"That was one way of getting rid of them," said Sarah as the fat man lumbered off the coach after Jean.

"Mm, I'm starting to worry about your bedside manner, Nurse Bradshaw."

Sarah laughed. "At least she can't remember I was rude to her last night – before cleaning her up, that is. I don't know what it is, but she brings out the worst in me. I'm so happy now Jason and I have made up, but she would try anyone's patience. I think she killed him, that's why she's so defensive."

"And what about Andrew Farmer? I thought you were convinced he did it." Rachel put her arm through Sarah's as they joined the queues to get on to the walkway. "Let's just hope she doesn't end up falling off this thing or you'll be in the frame for two murders."

During the spectacular walk, Rachel kept her eye on Max, who was head and shoulders taller than anyone else there and walked about ten metres ahead of them. His bright red helmet also made him stand out from the crowd

– Rachel supposed there might have been a problem finding one big enough to fit him. As she studied the rockface and the wooden platform they walked along, she wondered if there was a weight limit.

"I don't usually like heights, but this is wonderful," said Sarah. "It feels so sturdy underfoot."

Rachel was pleased to agree with her friend, as the walkway wasn't very wide and the gorge far below was barely visible. The rail also provided reassurance, and even without a guide, it would have been impossible to fall over the side without being thrown. She was pleased it was so busy as such malice would not go unnoticed.

Sarah kept stopping to take photographs and Rachel eventually lost sight of Max.

"Carlos would have enjoyed this."

"I'm sorry, Rachel. He'll be up and about again by the time we reach Corsica. You'll see."

"You're right. And by that time, I hope to have your cousin's murder solved so that I can enjoy the rest of my honeymoon—"

A piercing scream shattered the moment, echoing along the walls of the gorge.

# Chapter 24

Rumours were flying around the coach by the time Rachel and Sarah got back on board. They had been ushered along the platform at speed and the walkway was now closed off, as far as they could make out.

"What happened?" Sarah asked.

"A man fell over the side," answered an older passenger. "According to my friend, he was messing around and went over. I heard the scream, turned around and saw him crash on the rocks before falling into the water. Not a pleasant sight."

"Did you see who it was?"

"No, dear. Sorry."

Rachel and Sarah returned to the back of the coach. Max and Jean weren't there. They had been detained as possible witnesses, as far as Rachel could make out when they were rushed past her and Sarah. Duncan had been with them, but she had no idea where he'd appeared from, or when.

"Why do you think they stopped Max and the others?" asked Sarah.

"I was just thinking the same thing. They looked shocked. I've got a sinking feeling that might have been Luke who went over the side. I also saw Helena lurking in the background, but she was moved on by officials."

Sarah's mouth dropped open. "I didn't see any of that. I was too busy peering over the side, trying to see what had happened. Do you think he fell?"

Rachel had been trying to piece the small snippets of the scene she had witnessed together in her head. She and Sarah must only have been a couple of minutes behind the incident, but it had occurred beyond their vision around a bend. She only saw the aftermath, but from the look of terror on Jean's face and the shake of the head from Helena, warning Rachel not to acknowledge her, she knew who to ask later what had happened.

"I doubt he fell. Even if you were messing about, you would need to climb on to the rail to go over. Nope, I believe we have our second murder." She lowered her voice. "Helena knows what happened, I'm certain of that."

"Where did she appear from, and how could it have been Luke? He wasn't there."

"I saw Duncan with Max and Jean. He and Luke must have made their own way or got a different coach."

Passengers were murmuring about what had happened and Rachel suspected stories would be very much exaggerated by the time they got back to the ship.

"What's the delay?" a man called down to the driver, who shrugged his shoulders. They had been sitting on the coach for twenty minutes past the return time with still no sign of movement. Eventually, a couple of policemen appeared, followed by Max, Jean and Duncan, who all got on the coach. They joined Rachel and Sarah in silence, with Duncan taking the seat in front of the back row.

Jean appeared to forget about the animosity of earlier and grabbed Rachel, sobbing on her shoulder. Rachel let her cry, but raised a quizzical eyebrow to Max.

"Luke… erm, Luke fell over the side," he said with a cracked voice.

"How?" asked Sarah, as Jean was clinging on to Rachel so tightly she could barely breathe.

"We don't know," answered Duncan. "We were all preoccupied with the views and the fauna. The first I knew was when he screamed."

"Was that him screaming? I thought it was a woman," said Rachel, shifting in her seat a little to unravel herself from the distraught Jean.

"Jean screamed in unison," explained Max.

"I… I—" Jean tried to speak and Rachel took the opportunity to remove her newfound appendage from her shoulder, handing Jean some tissues to blow her nose. "I think he must have jumped. It all happened so quickly."

"Did no-one see what happened?" asked Rachel.

"We'd stopped to let a crowd of families go past; kids were running riot. Once we turned the bend, they were long gone, and it was blissfully quiet. We were enjoying the view, and then—"

Duncan stopped.

"There was a woman just behind us. I think she might have seen what happened, but she disappeared," said Max.

Duncan's head shot up. "What woman? I didn't see anyone else."

"You were looking over the rail by then. I noticed her earlier; she was ahead of us at first, but stopped to take some photos. A beautiful woman with long, dark, wavy hair, like a goddess."

Rachel nudged Sarah not to say anything. She knew who Max was referring to.

"I saw her too," said Jean. "I've seen her around the ship. Max's right. She might have seen what happened."

"But why didn't she stop?" asked Duncan.

"Perhaps she didn't see anything," said Rachel, fearing that Helena could be either involved in the untimely death, or in danger if one of these three was responsible for Luke going over the side. "You did say you had just turned a bend. Maybe she was still on the blind side. I expect she would have been as shocked as everyone else."

Duncan nodded. "That would explain it."

"What makes you think he jumped?" asked Sarah.

"He's been acting weird all week. He was devastated when Jean told him about the new salon opening up near him. He's done nothing but drink every day since Keith's death and has been downright morbid about everything. Last night, he picked up a guy in some group he went to, and by this morning, the guy had gone, along with Luke's cash and Rolex. He came crying at my door – that's why I thought we'd best join the tour and catch up with these guys. I hoped Max would sort him out, as he's his cousin. I'm no good with depressives."

"Poor Luke. He didn't say anything about any of that to me." Jean was perking up, having finished Rachel's packet of tissues.

"I wonder why." Duncan rolled his eyes.

"He didn't tell me either," said Max, "although we were both upset about the new salon. Keith never mentioned it to me and I'm his business partner."

"Yeah, well, you know what Keith was like. Loyalty wasn't his strong suit. Back to Luke, though. He'd cheered up by the time we got here – said he'd tap you for money, Max – and I thought he was over it. You know how moody he sometimes gets… um, got. He was up one minute, down the next. His emotions were all over the place. Hormonal, to say the least."

"Well obviously he wasn't over it, you ignoramus," snapped Jean.

"It didn't help you walking out on him last night, either, after flirting with him all evening," added Max.

"Hey! Don't blame me. Luke wasn't my type. We were friends, that's all. I like my men to be a bit more suave."

"Rich, you mean," spat Jean.

"And that. Look, whatever was going on, he'd obviously had enough. Keith's death seemed to tip him over the edge."

Jean's bleary eyes widened. "That's it. I get it now. I knew how angry Luke was with Keith over the salon; he said it would destroy him and vowed revenge. That explains everything."

"What are you saying?" asked Sarah.

"I'm saying, Nurse Death, that if you didn't kill Keith, then Luke did. It makes sense: Luke must have found Keith, they had a row and he killed him. Finding he couldn't live with himself after what he'd done, he ended it all."

Max tapped his fingers heavily on his knees. "No. I don't believe it. Luke wouldn't hurt anyone. He is – was – harmless."

Duncan ran his fingers through the curly black hair falling over his face. "Jean's on to something there. It does make sense. Now you mention it, he did leave in a huff the night Keith died. He'd had a skinful and was raging mad about the salon. I just put it down to his seesawing hormones, but what if he did come upon Keith? They argued and he hit him over the head with the fire extinguisher. It does explain it."

Sarah nudged Rachel and whispered, "It makes sense to me. Waverley will be delighted. Apart from the death of another passenger, that is. I can't wait to tell Jason."

Rachel nodded, but remained silent, weighing what she'd heard up in her head. It made for a neat and tidy resolution to the investigation into Keith Bird's death. She could accept it and get on with her honeymoon.

*So why the nagging doubt?*

\*\*\*

Waverley stood overseeing passengers being scanned through the security entrance to board the ship. He nodded to Rachel and Sarah.

"Welcome back. An eventful day again, ladies. Excuse me."

Rachel didn't have the opportunity to reply, as Waverley's attention swiftly moved elsewhere. Max, Duncan and Jean had been directed to one side and the security chief headed their way. She watched as they were led away, presumably to Waverley's office where they could give an account of the death of their companion.

"I'm so pleased it's all over, Rachel. Come on, let's get tea in Creams, and then go and tell Carlos the good news."

"Good to see you've got your priorities right," said Rachel. "Although I am a bit peckish. I could murder a cinnamon roll right now."

"Choose your words carefully," Sarah laughed.

Sarah chatted away happily all through tea while Rachel listened. It was great to see her friend happy again, even if she herself wasn't entirely convinced that Luke murdered Keith, and then took his own life. She wished she could accept what appeared to be an obvious conclusion, but the nagging doubt in her gut just wouldn't go away. Having no desire to burst Sarah's bubble without any evidence to the contrary, she decided not to.

"Come on, Sarah, time's up. I want to see my husband."

Sarah gulped down the last of her tea, and they both headed down to the medical centre and the infirmary. Carlos seemed agitated, and before Rachel had any opportunity to say anything, he swung his legs over the edge of the bed.

"Where have you been? I've been calling you for the past hour."

He *was* agitated. It wasn't like him to police her movements, so she let it go.

"We went to Creams. Sorry, Sarah was hungry."

He puffed out his cheeks in disgust, then began throwing himself around on the bed.

"Carlos, what's the matter?"

"Helena's gone missing. I can't reach her. I need to get out of this place." He reached towards his drip, ready to pull it out.

"Oh no you don't." Sarah grabbed his hand with great speed, considering she had just eaten the largest cream cake available in the patisserie. She looked at Rachel. "He's burning up again. His blood pressure's through the roof. Carlos, do you feel confused?"

Brigitte appeared from the treatment room, armed with the next dose of antibiotic.

"Thank God you're here. I've paged Graham. He's been ranting for the past half-hour. I can't make any sense of it."

Rachel helped Carlos back into bed.

"Everything's fine, darling. Sarah and I saw Helena at the Caminito del Rey. She's okay, Carlos."

Carlos slumped back on his pillow.

"Are you sure?"

"Yes, darling. Please rest. Dr Bentley's on his way."

Carlos muttered something unintelligible about Helena being in danger and walking into a trap. Nothing he said made any sense. Rachel's heart rate felt like it was going into overdrive as she watched her husband growing weaker before her eyes. The monitors were showing a high blood pressure, rapid pulse and raging temperature.

Dr Bentley arrived just before Carlos passed out. Panic swept through Rachel's veins as she watched the doctor and nurses rapidly assess Carlos's vitals.

"He's tachycardic," said Dr Bentley.

"What happened?"

"I don't know," said Brigitte. "He was getting agitated. Brillo popped in after her shore leave, so I asked her to check him over while I went to get the next dose of antibiotic and page you. When I got back, Sarah and Rachel were here and he was worse."

"Where is Brillo now?" Dr Bentley shouted.

"I don't know." Brigitte seemed worried. "His obs are worse."

"There was no sign of her when we came in," said Sarah.

"Never mind that now. He's going into septic shock. We need to treat him urgently. Rachel, I really should call for an ambulance to take him to hospital. It's serious."

Rachel was torn. Carlos had been adamant he didn't want to go to a hospital on land, but she couldn't bear it if he died because she refused. She nodded.

"Call it."

"No, don't," came a voice from the door. They turned to see Helena standing there. "His antibiotics have been tampered with. You've been giving him cocaine. I'm not sure how many doses he's had."

Dr Bentley's eyes widened. His face reddened.

"How could that happen, and how do you know?"

"I found these in a passenger's room, and it all added up." Helena handed three vials of powder to Dr Bentley. "These are the real bottles. Squirt a bit of that on my finger." She spoke to Brigitte, nodding towards the syringe the nurse had been about to inject into Carlos's line. Dr Bentley nodded for Brigitte to do as she was asked. Helena dipped her finger into the substance and licked a tiny bit.

"Raw cocaine. Another dose and he would have been dead. As it is, if you run fluids through him, you'll flush his system. He won't be any worse for wear in a few hours, as long as he responds." Helena looked at Rachel. "I promise you, they will pay for this. Trust me."

Stunned silence filled the room after Helena left.

"Who was that woman?" asked Dr Bentley.

"She's the one Carlos has been working with. She didn't say who did the switch," Rachel said finally, fighting the urge to run after Helena, but Carlos was her top priority at that moment.

"It explains the temperature and blood pressure. Let's get this saline drip run through fast. Give him a dose of the right stuff, Brigitte. I'll also need IV benzos. Lorazepam will do."

"Yes, sir." Brigitte hurried back to the treatment room to draw up the antibiotic. Dr Bentley increased the saline drip to let it flush through fast and Rachel watched the monitor to check the response. Carlos's blood pressure was still high, but his heart rate lowered.

"Why benzodiazepines?" she asked.

"It'll reduce the agitation he's been feeling and lower the blood pressure," Dr Bentley explained before injecting the syringe Brigitte had brought into the IV line.

Half an hour later, Carlos's condition had stabilised, and he slept. Dr Bentley had called Waverley, who was marching impatiently up and down outside the infirmary in heated conversation with the chief medical officer.

Rachel refused to talk to the security chief until she'd had time to speak to Carlos, and she also refused to wake him.

His brown eyes opened at last and he gazed into her tear-filled blue ones.

"That was close."

She smiled grimly.

# Chapter 25

After spending time with Carlos to check he was back to normal, Rachel reluctantly allowed Waverley to join them. Dr Bentley also took a seat at the bedside, along with Sarah and Jason.

Rachel laughed ruefully. "This scene brings back terrible memories, but last time it was me lying in that bed."

"I owe you an enormous apology, Carlos. I have no idea how any drugs in the medical centre could have been swapped, but I have every intention of finding out." Dr Bentley's mortified tone said it all.

"It wasn't your fault, Doctor," said Carlos. "These people are cunning and devious. They can get in anywhere."

"What people?" asked Dr Bentley.

"Let's start at the beginning, shall we?" suggested Waverley. "As you know, Carlos here was shot yesterday while in Cadiz. It turns out he was assisting an Italian security service agent investigate a rogue terrorist cell, some of whom are on board this ship."

Dr Bentley's brow furrowed. "The agent was that lady who turned up here just in time?"

"Yes," answered Rachel. "Her name's Helena. Carlos has worked with her in the past."

Waverley coughed, indicating it was time for him to take over the story.

"As I was saying, there are one if not two members of the cell on board. Carlos filled Goodridge and me in on the situation this morning. He and this agent known as Helena believe that a government minister called Andrew Farmer is the go-between for a deal that's due to take place soon, if it hasn't already done so. The attempt on Carlos's life yesterday shows that Helena's cover may have been blown or, as she believes, it was a warning to back off. We do have one person in the brig who will be handed over to the authorities in Corsica in a few days' time, but no evidence he was part of the cell as yet. Helena invented a crime for which this man was arrested. Carlos and Helena believe there are two cells on board, one unaware of the other. They did believe the first cell consists of the man in the brig and the man who shot Carlos, but it now appears there is a third party involved in that cell."

"Why two cells?" asked Rachel.

"It's standard Mafioso tactics," said Carlos. "One cell watches over the other to make sure everything goes smoothly. It also ensures no-one backs out, because if they do, they are silenced."

"Mafia?" asked Dr Bentley, mouth opening wide. "What have they got to do with this?"

"Everything," said Carlos. "There's a rogue group who have moved into London and are behind lots of large construction deals. They use parent companies to hide their true identity and weed out corrupt officials or those they can blackmail or terrorise into helping. It appears Andrew Farmer has expensive tastes – or rather, his wife does – kids in private school, all that sort of thing. He was an easy target."

"Now we need to discover who Farmer is dealing with and who the third member of the other cell is," Waverley announced.

"I've got a sneaky suspicion I'm not going to like what you find. My junior went missing when she was supposed to be looking after Carlos," said Dr Bentley. "And does any of this have anything to do with the death of Keith Bird?"

"No. That case is solved. It appears one of his friends killed him and committed suicide today. You may have heard about the jumper."

Rachel was still mulling over whether Dr Sin could be involved in the attack on her husband. She would have been able to access the medicines with ease.

"Ah, yes, a Mr Luke Connelly. Brillo mentioned it when she got back from shore leave. I asked her to cover for me while I went to see Captain Jenson, but I didn't realise she would come here. Where is that woman, by the way? Even if she's not involved in this conspiracy, I need to speak to her about why she left an ill patient alone in the infirmary."

Waverley was about to reply when Rachel stopped everyone.

"Shush. Can you hear that?"

The sound of shuffling came from the laundry room at the end of the infirmary. Dr Bentley walked towards it.

"Wait. Stand back," commanded Jason, reaching for his taser. He unlocked the door and peered inside before opening the door wide and switching the light on.

There, sitting on the floor with hands tied in front of her and a handkerchief over her mouth, was the wild-haired Brillo Sin, trying to yell through the gag. Brigitte turned away to disguise the smirk on her face and Sarah had to do the same. Jason untied the junior doctor's hands and removed the gag.

"About time too! What do you call this? Some silly prank has been played on me by one of your so-called nurses. They should all be fired. I'm going straight to the captain. This ship is the most disorganised, disrespectful—"

The tirade went on for around five minutes. No amount of consolation was going to stop the furious doctor sounding off and letting all of them know what she felt about their 'abysmal excuse for a ship'. Rachel doubled up laughing with her head on Carlos's bed. Waverley and Dr

Bentley did their utmost to quieten the woman's rant and Brigitte giggled into her computer screen. It took Gwen's appearance to assist with the irate doctor before she and Dr Bentley could get Brillo Sin out of the infirmary and shuffle her towards the senior nurse's office.

"Well," said Waverley, "I don't think I've ever encountered anyone quite like Dr Sin before."

"Really? That's her on a good day," said Brigitte. "She's a ray of sunshine."

Even Waverley chuckled before staring at Brigitte.

"You didn't?"

"Of course not. What do you take me for? Although if I'd thought of it, I might have been tempted. She's the doctor from hell. Can't you arrest her for abuse and insubordination or something?"

"Under the circumstances, we must let her believe it was a silly prank. We can't tell her that she was locked up by a member of a terrorist organisation, can we?" Waverley giggled. "I wonder who will take the blame."

The smile left Brigitte's face. "I was the one down here with her. I left her with Carlos. She's bound to blame me. She already hates me. It's not fair."

"You should think of that next time you're tempted to lock away a senior officer in a laundry cupboard," laughed Sarah.

"Bernard's going to love this," said Brigitte.

"Helena!" Carlos cried out suddenly from his bed. Rachel's head shot up.

"What?"

"It's coming back to me; I was in a haze. A man dressed in scrubs and a mask attacked Dr Sin. He said he'd kill her if I moved from the bed while he locked her away. Then he drugged me. He told me Helena was next, that they'd set a trap for her and there was nothing I could do about it."

"That must have been the first dose of cocaine," said Sarah. "Then he switched more cocaine for Carlos's next dose of medication."

"Rachel," Carlos's voice was urgent, "you have to find her. Save her."

"I will, Carlos. I promise." Turning to Waverley, Rachel glared. "Don't even try to stop me. She saved my husband's life. I owe her."

"In that case, I suggest we start with Mr Farmer. The ship's about to depart, according to the captain's announcement just now, so he should be on board. Goodridge, I suggest you make sure Gwen and Dr Bentley go along with the prank thing with the new doctor, then check on Ms—?"

"De Luca," offered Carlos.

"Ms Helena De Luca. Also circulate her picture among the security team. If the culprits plan to throw her overboard, they won't do it while passengers are viewing our port departure, so we have an hour or so to find her."

"Yes, sir," said Jason.

Rachel kissed Carlos on the forehead.

"We *will* find her."

"Don't worry about him. I'll get changed and relieve Brigitte. Then I'll stick to him like glue," said Sarah.

Waverley paused and turned to Carlos, who had flopped back on his pillow, eyes closed. He shrugged.

"Let's go. We're going to look damned silly if she's sunbathing on her balcony."

"I'll keep phoning her room," offered Brigitte. "My patient's stable for now and I want to help."

The commotion inside Gwen's office continued and Jason sighed as he knocked. Rachel gave him a wink.

"Good luck."

\*\*\*

Farmer didn't answer his door, so Waverley let himself in with his shipwide pass. The room was empty except for the smell of cigar smoke. Waverley scrunched up his nose.

"Damn stuff reeks worse than cigarette smoke. I bet he's been smoking on the balcony. Idiot."

Rachel was aware that every crew member's dread was a fire aboard a cruise ship. While ships were fitted with state-of-the-art sprinklers and fire doors, an unchecked fire could result in multiple deaths. There were very few designated smoking zones, and none of them were in passenger quarters.

"The smell could just be from his clothes," she said. "Aren't smoke alarms fitted on the balconies?"

"They can be blocked," growled Waverley. "If I find out he's blocked it and smoked on the balcony, his butler will be gone."

Feeling it was time to move on from the smoking thing, Rachel suggested they have a look around. Knowing there was money in the suitcase under the bed, she headed through to the bedroom. Sarah's ferret in Farmer's room was unknown to Waverley, so she opened and closed drawers to make a show of rummaging before pulling out the heavy suitcase.

"Look here!"

Waverley joined her in the bedroom and let out a low whistle.

"That confirms that a deal is going down, but has he been paid, or is he doing the paying?"

"I guess we'll find out soon enough."

They were leaving the bedroom when a key card was inserted the other side of the entrance door. Waverley stood to one side as Farmer entered.

"Mr Farmer, just the person we were looking for. Do come in." Waverley's voice was calm, but insistent.

The initial fear and shock passing briefly over Farmer's face turned to a quizzical expression.

"Who are you? What are you doing in my room?"

"Forgive me. I'm chief of security Jack Waverley. This is Rachel Prince, an undercover police officer," he winked at Rachel. "We would like to speak with you about some of your, erm, business dealings."

Rachel had to give it to Farmer, he was ice-cold under the circumstances, giving nothing away. He sucked his lips in before answering.

"Of course. How can I be of help? Have I been robbed?"

"No, sir. You have not been robbed, but you should be careful about leaving large amounts of cash in an unlocked suitcase under your bed."

Rachel gauged Farmer's reaction. His bulldog face frowned temporarily, but he regained a smarmy composure.

"I'm not sure what gives you the right to rifle through my belongings, but it is not illegal to carry cash, as far as I'm aware. I don't always trust credit cards – too many scams, you know."

Tired of prancing around, Waverley pulled a phone out of his pocket and showed a photo of Helena to Farmer.

"Do you recognise this woman?"

The quick dart of the eyes told Rachel he did.

"No. Never seen her before. A pretty little thing, though. I'd be happy to meet her." He sucked his lips in again. His arrogance got to Rachel and she snapped.

"Where is she?"

"I've told you, I don't know her. How should I know where she is?"

Waverley shot her a quick warning look before playing good cop.

"Perhaps if you help us, we can help you. You see, one of my security officers has in his possession papers that implicate you in taking bribes from the Mafia."

Farmer's mouth dropped open, sweat appeared on his forehead and he slumped down in a chair.

"The Mafia? What are you talking about?" he asked, breathlessly.

Rachel took over. "The company you have given large construction contracts to is a cover for a Mafia cell that intends on carrying out terrorist attacks in London and Rome. I don't think the Prime Minister is going to be one of your Facebook friends on your return to England, but MI6 are extremely interested in meeting you."

Farmer took out a handkerchief and wiped sweat from his brow. His eyes darted between Rachel and Waverley. She could almost see his cogs moving, trying to worm his way out of the scrape he had got himself in.

"I'm housing minister, I sign contracts all the time. How am I supposed to know if one of the contractors is crooked? You can't prove anything."

"Perhaps not, but we can certainly imply it. We do have evidence of bribes, so you may as well realise your political career is over. The kids might have to go to state school. Such a shame."

Rachel smiled at Waverley; it was his turn.

"If you're willing to help us put these people away, we can make sure it's not leaked you ratted on the Mafia."

"But I don't know anything about the Mafia."

"We can make sure that everyone believes you knew exactly what you were getting into." Rachel dealt the death blow and the man crumbled.

"Okay. What do you want me to do?"

# Chapter 26

Carlos dragged himself out of bed once Sarah had relieved Brigitte.

"Please, Sarah, take this thing out." He pointed to the IV line.

"I can't, Carlos. You need to rest."

"Sarah, I'm leaving with your help or without it. I'll sign any papers you have and take full responsibility, but I have to help. I can't lie here while my wife is out there searching for a killer."

Sarah sighed heavily. She switched off the intravenous fluid running through and disconnected the line before covering the cannula with a dressing.

"I'm leaving this in because you still need intravenous antibiotics when you get over this madness." She pulled the curtains. "I'll let you get dressed while I call Jason. You can go together or not at all."

"I can live with that, but tell him to be quick."

Jason was standing outside the curtains by the time Carlos was dressed.

"That was quick."

"Are you sure about this, mate? You still seem a bit peaky to me."

"I'm sure." Carlos stood up and grabbed Jason's arm as the room spun. He took deep breaths to get himself reoriented. "Why do people do this to themselves?"

"Crack, you mean?" asked Jason.

"Yes."

"It's supposed to give you a high, mate."

"Well, it's not working." Carlos forced himself to stand upright and nodded. "Okay, I'm ready."

It was harder than he'd imagined keeping pace with Jason, and he had to keep shaking his head to get rid of the weird stuff and differentiate hallucination from reality. Jason was still a white blur, but with every step, Carlos felt closer to helping the woman he loved most in the world and the woman who was forever saving his life. Jason helped him into the lift, and he was relieved to lean against the wall.

"Where are we heading?" he asked.

"Helena's room. I was just there when Sarah called. She's not there, but there might be clues. Maybe she left us something to go on."

"She will have. She's bright and would have anticipated this scenario. Where's Rachel?"

"With the boss. They went to question Andrew Farmer."

"Ah, the dirty, greasy bulldog-faced soon-to-be ex-minister," said Carlos.

They arrived on the eighth deck and were soon inside Helena's room thanks to Jason's universal passkey. The scent was Helena's: Christian Dior, her favourite perfumer. Carlos remembered it from working with her. The room was tidy, no signs of a struggle. Wherever she was, she hadn't been taken from here.

"I'll check the safe," Jason suggested.

"You'll never guess her password."

"I don't need to. I'm security, I can override every safe on board this ship with my own code. Every one of us has our own, so if any of us turned out to be criminals, the boss would know who it was."

"Good to know," said Carlos, taking a seat while checking drawers at the dressing table. It felt strange going through Helena's things and he had to force himself to do it.

"Nothing in here but passport, cash and jewellery." Jason sounded disappointed.

Carlos sat back in the chair. "Think, think," he told himself, wishing the clouds would remove themselves from his head.

Jason poured them each a glass of water.

"Here, drink this. You need to stay hydrated. Sarah's orders. It might help you concentrate."

Carlos did as requested and stared into space.

"Turn the TV on," he told Jason.

"Are you still hallucinating? This is no time to be watching television."

"Seriously. Turn it on."

Jason took the remote and pointed it at the television. Nothing happened.

"It's not working."

"We need a screwdriver set."

Realisation crossed over Jason's face as he jumped up from the bed.

"I'll find one of the engineers and borrow one. Wait there."

Carlos turned the television around and noted the screws were scratched. He smiled to himself through the smog of drug-fuelled dysfunction.

"Clever girl."

Jason had the back off in no time and retrieved the memory card from behind it. Helena had most likely fused the television from the plug to protect the card and asked the stateroom attendant to leave it off. They took the card down to Waverley's office, where they found Waverley and Rachel hatching a plan.

Rachel's jaw dropped when she saw Carlos, but she nodded a greeting, having the good sense to recognise that she would have done the same thing if the tables were turned. The security chief was not quite so understanding.

"What's going on, Goodridge?"

Ignoring the question, Jason handed over the memory card.

"We found this in Ms De Luca's room, sir. It was behind the back of the TV. I never would have found it without Carlos, sir."

"Right." Waverley's face softened as he looked at Carlos. "You'd better take a seat before you fall down."

"Thank you. I think I will."

Jason poured water from the water dispenser and handed it to Carlos while Waverley and Rachel joined them around a coffee table in the centre of the security chief's office.

"You do the honours." Waverley handed his laptop to Carlos, along with the memory card. Carlos turned the screen to show what was on the card. There were files with dates and times since Helena had boarded the ship. Each one revealed what she had uncovered, including the meeting with Rachel and the documents found in Jean Sutton's room.

"Of course, Jean Sutton!" shouted Rachel. "She had these files and a key to Keith's room. I think Keith picked these papers up in the salon. Maybe Farmer left his briefcase or document wallet. Keith circled names he must have recognised as Mafia – Luke mentioned something about Keith being neurotic about the Mafia, and with his clientele, I'm betting Keith found out long ago who to avoid dealing with. Any other time, he would have blackmailed Farmer, but this was out of his league. He panicked, turned and ran, hoping no-one would link him to the documents if Farmer found out they were missing. He probably planned to lie low to see if anything came of it, which was why he applied for a job on board a cruise ship."

"But Jean Sutton found the documents and decided to make some money on the side," Waverley continued. "Perhaps she tried to get Keith Bird to play ball, and when he refused, she killed him."

"That puts paid to the fact Luke Connelly killed him out of revenge, and then killed himself," Jason groaned.

"Who? What?" asked Carlos.

"I didn't get the chance to tell you earlier because you were so ill," said Rachel. "Luke went over the side at Caminito del Rey today. Everyone assumed it was suicide, and Jean suggested Luke may have killed Keith after an argument about a rival salon that he'd set up. It made some sense, but I couldn't believe Luke was a murderer. He was too soft. Now I think we should assume that Luke knew something and was murdered too."

"Why didn't you say before that you didn't think Luke was the killer?" snapped Waverley.

"Because I wasn't sure. If I'm honest, I hoped it would be as simple as that so Carlos and I could get on with our honeymoon." Her shoulders sagged as the elation she'd felt a few moments earlier subsided. "I don't have Jean down as a blackmailer, or a murderer. From what I've gathered, Keith didn't trust her, so she wouldn't have recognised the significance of the names he had circled anyway."

"So you think the murder of Keith and this spy ring or whatever it is are linked?" Waverley stroked his hairline.

"Oh yes. To me, the documents in Keith's folder confirm that. It must have been what he wanted to talk to me about. But I'm still not certain about the who."

"It has to be Jean Sutton, seeing as she was in possession of the folder." Waverley's neck reddened. He was becoming exasperated. Carlos felt it was time to move things along.

"Let's see if this stuff Helena uncovered gives us any more clues." He opened up the documents one by one.

"Wait. Stop. Scroll back," said Rachel.

Carlos scrolled through photos taken of when he and Helena had met over coffee while Rachel was with Sarah the morning after Keith died.

"There we have our third person from the cell that tried to kill you." Rachel pointed to the man clearly watching over the meeting.

"Who is he?"

"Pierre Dewandre," said Jason. "He works in Coral Hair and Beauty."

"Of course," said Rachel. "He showed far too much interest in Keith and his interview with his boss, Esther Jarvis. He'd obviously been tipped off as to why Keith was on board. Esther tried to warn me Keith had been frightened and to stay out of it. Perhaps she suspects Pierre of something."

"Is he our killer?" asked Carlos.

"Let's go and find out," said Waverley, understandably itching to get results.

"Perhaps Jason and I should go and speak to Jean Sutton while you do that," suggested Rachel.

Waverley nodded. "Let's question them separately and meet back here in an hour."

Carlos was worried. "We still need to find Helena. Time's not on our side."

Rachel squeezed his arm. "We will."

# Chapter 27

J ean wasn't in her room when Jason and Rachel arrived. Clothes were scattered about and a pile of used tissues were in the bin. They rummaged through drawers, the safe and Jean's belongings, but came up with nothing. The only thing they had was the document wallet and the key to Keith's room.

"Looks like she's gone down for dinner. There's no evidence Helena's been near here," Rachel said, disappointed. She was as anxious as Carlos was about Helena. Her husband would blame himself if anything happened to his friend, and she felt indebted to the woman who had saved Carlos's life.

"She's untidy, isn't she?"

"Let's hope that's her only crime." Rachel's thoughts returned to the night she and Sarah had brought the drunken Jean back to her room. Was it really only yesterday? Now she thought of it, something was odd, but she couldn't decide what it was. "It was messy last night when we brought her back plastered. I don't envy the stateroom steward. Let's try the bars, I'm sure she'll be having pre-dinner drinks."

They decided to split up, with Jason going through deck six and Rachel deck five. Rachel saw Jean in the Wine Bar. She was pleased to find her alone.

"Do you mind if I join you?"

Jean raised her head nonchalantly. "It's a free country, or should I say ship?"

It was obvious the woman had already had a skinful, so Rachel decided to get straight to the point to avoid a repeat of the night before. She placed the document wallet on the table and pushed it towards Jean, whose head shot up in surprise.

"That's Keith's. What are you doing with it?"

"I'd like to ask you the same thing. Last night when you kindly offered to lend me a pair of shorts, I found this and a key to Keith's room in your dressing table drawer."

"What? I don't know what you're talking about. This is Keith's personal document wallet. No-one was allowed to touch it, and as for a key to his room, you've got to be kidding. He wouldn't have given me or anyone else a key."

"I didn't say he gave you the key. I'm suggesting you might have taken it off him after you killed him, and then stole the wallet from his room."

Jean's face turned crimson. "You must be mad if you think I had anything to do with Keith's death." The squeaky voice had risen to a screech. "And as for the wallet, I didn't even know Keith had it with him. I thought he would have left it in the safe in the salon where he always kept it. I haven't seen it on the cruise, and I'm telling you again, I did not kill him. Why would I?"

"Because you discovered he was going to sack you. Or perhaps because of what's in that file."

"That's just hearsay; Keith wouldn't have sacked me. He needed me. Anyway, I knew too much about his dealings and some of his so-called clients."

"So you would have resorted to blackmail?"

"If necessary. So you see, I had no reason to kill him."

"What about the names and deals in the file? You knew he had found out what Andrew Farmer was up to. You wanted to blackmail the minister. Maybe Keith wouldn't go along with it or wouldn't give you a cut."

"Andrew Farmer the politician? What the hell has he got to do with anything? You're crazy." Jean took a slug of red wine from her glass, barely allowing it to go down before she leaned towards Rachel, so close Rachel could almost taste the wine from the woman's breath. "Luke killed Keith in a fit of rage, and then killed himself. Why are you trying to pin this on me?"

"Luke didn't kill Keith. In fact, he was murdered himself, and you were conveniently close to him on the platform, from what I can gather. Now tell me, where's Helena?"

Jean's eyes bulged as she pulled herself up to loom over Rachel.

"Luke murdered? What is this, Happy Hour? I know what's going on. Your friend killed Keith, and now you're clubbing together to pin it on me. Well, you can't because I didn't do it. DO YOU HEAR?"

Jean somehow managed to push herself to an upright position and stagger out of the bar. A few heads had turned in Rachel's direction, and she smiled and shrugged as she made her way back to Waverley's office. She hoped Waverley and Carlos had had more luck than she had. The clock was ticking and she felt certain that whoever was holding Helena would dispose of her after dark, most probably over the side. She just hoped they hadn't already killed her.

Was it possible that the two crimes weren't linked at all? That Keith's death had been more personal, and Rachel had been sidetracked by the terrorist thing Helena and Carlos were investigating? If so, Pierre might be the only link to finding Helena, and Keith's murder could wait.

She got to Waverley's office. Jason was already there.

"I saw you had found Jean Sutton and didn't like to interrupt your, erm, interrogation."

"It was rather like that."

"So where is she?"

"No idea. She stormed off, so if she doesn't pass out, she'll be heading for dinner soon."

"You don't seem disappointed."

"She didn't do it. She had no idea about the wallet, or the key, and I believe her. They were a plant. I was trying to work out what had been bothering me and it was that the room was an absolute mess, along with every drawer, but in this one drawer, a folder and key were placed in meticulous alignment."

"Ah. So we're no closer to finding Helena De Luca?"

Waverley and Carlos arrived at that moment, alongside a dishevelled Pierre.

"Sit!" Waverley commanded. Pierre obeyed.

"We think it was Farmer all along," said Carlos. "According to Pierre here, Farmer's linked to big business."

"But we know that, and I'm sure he's dirty if those names in that file are indeed Mafia, so what's new?"

Carlos's eyes bored into Pierre's. "Farmer has Helena somewhere."

"But we searched his room," said Rachel.

"Speak, man," Waverley commanded.

Pierre licked his dry lips. "I'm just a watchman. I get paid to watch people, that's all. I don't ask questions. Mr Farmer approached me at the beginning of the cruise to let him know about the movements of certain people. One was the woman who met with this man," he pointed to Carlos, "and the other was Keith Bird. He said Mr Bird had stolen documents from him and he wanted to retrieve them. I don't know what documents he wanted, or why.

And I don't know anything about any Mafia." Pierre's eyes widened.

Rachel's thoughts jumbled once again as she tried to work out the significance of Pierre's words.

"I had no idea anyone would get killed. Mr Farmer paid me for information and told me to keep my mouth shut."

"Anything else?"

"I stole a key from Mr Bird and gave it to Mr Farmer, that's all."

"She's in Keith's room!" shouted Rachel.

They leapt into action. Waverley called another security officer to stay with Pierre while they ran up to deck eight. Rachel could see it was getting dark outside and hoped they would be in time. Waverley placed his key card in the door, but had no time to enter as Carlos barged past with renewed vigour and burst into the room.

Andrew Farmer was dragging a tied and gagged Helena towards the opened balcony doors. Carlos raced forwards and punched the man hard in the face, causing him to reel backwards. Jason took over and applied cuffs while Rachel untied Helena.

"Are you okay?"

Helena nodded. "A bit dazed. He drugged me, and when I came round, I was being dragged towards the balcony. Thank you."

Carlos joined Rachel and helped Helena into a chair. Farmer sucked blood from his mouth where Carlos had hit him.

Scowling at Carlos, he said, "How did you survive?"

"That was down to my friend here," he handed Helena a bottle of water from the refrigerator in Keith's room. "She worked out you'd switched my antibiotics for cocaine. I expect cocaine smuggling will be added to your list of crimes. What made you think you'd get away with murder? You could have gone quietly."

"I was going to finish off Miss Nosy Parker here, and then get off in Ajaccio and make my way to Italy. I have connections there and I could have started a new life under a different name. I still could. I don't suppose you guys are open to offers? I can make you extremely rich."

"Slimy to the end," said Rachel. "What about your wife and children?"

"What about them, Miss Righteous Pants? It was a marriage of convenience. She got the house and lifestyle she wanted. The kids got private schooling, and I got to play away from home."

"With the likes of Duncan Fairchild. She turned a blind eye to your indiscretions while you played the field. I'm surprised some sleazy newspaper hasn't picked up your double life."

"Oh, who cares about such things these days? I'm saying no more until I speak to a lawyer."

Waverley proceeded with charging him.

"Andrew Farmer, I'm arresting you on two charges of attempted murder and bribing a crew member. You will be kept in the brig until we return to Southampton, where we will hand you over to the port authorities, and I will also hand over the dossier from the document folder and any information Miss De Luca has found in the course of her investigation. We'll leave the British and Italian police to fight over who wants you the most. Your little syndicate is already under investigation by MI6, and with Miss De Luca's assistance it will be closed down."

"With a good lawyer, I'll be out in five years. Don't think you've heard the last of Andrew Farmer. I'll hunt your little band down and put an end to it. I should have ordered a shoot-to-kill on you." He glared at Carlos, sending a shiver down Rachel's spine. "My mistake. It won't happen the next time, and as for you," he now focussed on Helena, "keep looking over your shoulder. Your days are numbered."

Waverley had clearly had enough.

"Take him away, Goodridge."

"Will he really be out in five years?" asked Rachel.

"Not a chance," said Waverley. "MI6 will make sure he's classed as a dangerous terrorist. He'll be lucky if he gets out in twenty."

"And then the Italian government will rearrest him and charge him with inciting terrorism and collaborating with the Mafia," said Helena. "If he tries to do a deal, the Mafia will get him before anyone else. I won't be looking over my shoulder anytime soon. I also discovered the leak inside our agency and that has been plugged. I found the name on Farmer's phone, and the money he was carrying is counterfeit. He has no idea the storm he's about to be hit with."

Rachel sighed and kissed Carlos.

"It's time you were back in hospital. If you're good, and Sarah lets me, I'll stay the night."

# Chapter 28

All was quiet in the infirmary when Rachel arrived after dinner. Carlos was sleeping off his drug-induced haze and Sarah sat reading.

"How's the patient?" she asked.

"Exhausted," Sarah whispered. "I'm so pleased he's out of danger and Helena's safe. I told you it was Farmer."

Rachel decided not to point out that Farmer was not responsible for Keith's death, as it would be churlish.

"You did, and what a viper he turned out to be. He obviously cased the medical centre when he came down that night with his self-induced asthma attack."

"What I don't understand is why he tried to kill Carlos when he could have had him killed first time round."

"That puzzles me too. The only thing I can think of is that Helena was getting too close for comfort and he decided to get rid of anyone associated with the investigation. When he needed a room to keep Helena in until he could do away with her, he remembered he had the key to Keith's. It was perfect, and he would have got away with it if it hadn't been for Helena's thorough notes and photos."

"How did she manage to get photos of Pierre watching her?"

"She wore a brooch containing a hidden video recorder. Each night, she downloaded the footage to her laptop and took stills of anyone of interest. Some were innocent bystanders, but others, like Pierre and the other man following her, were watching her. She wasn't convinced about Pierre, but he was the missing link, albeit an unknowing one who had no idea what he was involved with."

Carlos turned over in his sleep, but was dead to the world.

"How did Farmer know about Pierre and his little money-making sideline?"

"How do any of these criminals find contacts? Word of mouth, probably. At least that case is solved."

"What do you mean? Didn't Farmer kill or have Keith killed?"

"Nope. Definitely not; all he wanted was his document wallet back. For all he knew, Keith wouldn't recognise the names Farmer was dealing with as Mafia."

"How can you be so sure, Rachel? It has to have been him. Keith had the documents, and you said yourself he wanted them back."

"Yes, but Farmer wouldn't have planted those documents in Jean's room, would he? The idea was to frame Jean for murdering Keith, not to bring the ceiling down on his own misdemeanours."

Sarah's hand went to her mouth as she bit her lip.

"You're right. I thought it was all Farmer, so I was wrong all along."

"Not entirely. You knew he was a slimeball and up to no good, and he was. Actually, he's more dangerous than the person who killed Keith."

"So was it Luke after all?"

Rachel had been racking her brains for answers on this one, but no matter how hard she tried, she couldn't find out who'd killed Keith Bird. It had to be the most annoying case she'd investigated so far, and she was no closer to finding out who did it.

"That's one theory."

"Or it could have been Jean and the folder wasn't planted in her room?" Sarah looked hopeful.

"That's another theory."

"But?"

"I could just about understand her hanging on to the documents if she was planning to make a little money on the side, but why not put them in the safe? And why hang on to the key?"

"She's not the brightest, though, is she? With the amount she drinks, I'm surprised she gets anything done. I don't think sense is part of her nature."

"I'd like it to be her as much as you would, but I think she genuinely liked, maybe loved Keith. The look on her face when I challenged her about the documents was genuine surprise – she even accused me of trying to frame her to protect you. And remember, she's a gossip. She wouldn't be able to resist telling someone about her find if she'd read those papers. And we don't know whether she's drinking more because of the loss of Keith and now Luke, or just because she's on holiday. People do. Trust me, I know. Remember I used to walk the streets of London as a PC."

Sarah stood up to check Carlos's monitors and write down observations on his charts, and then rejoined Rachel at the nurses' desk.

"So who do you think it was, Sherlock?"

"I don't know. It's so frustrating. One minute I think it *was* Luke, then I wonder if it was Max, but the motive is weak. Then Duncan, but he has no grudge against Keith as far as I can fathom. Esther Jarvis is an outside guess, but that's it. They're all guesses. What I need is evidence."

"Perhaps when you stop thinking about it, it will come to you. Now Carlos is safe, your mind is free to concentrate. I reckon it was Luke if Keith wasn't killed for the documents."

Rachel pondered on this. It could be that simple, but she couldn't shake off the idea that she was missing something obvious. She was convinced Jean wasn't the killer because she had been genuinely shocked when

Rachel confronted her with the document wallet and the key to Keith's room. Whoever it was had to be one of the other three, because who else would want to frame Jean? If Luke had been murdered and Jean wasn't responsible, there remained the two suspects with the weakest motives.

"You know what? I need a drink. Are you off soon? While Carlos's asleep, we could go to the Jazz Bar."

Sarah's face lit up. "Now you're talking." She checked her watch. "Bernard should be along any minute."

"Did I hear my name mentioned?" The happy face of the wonderful Bernard beamed at the two women. "And I hear you solved another murder mystery, Mrs Jacobi-Prince." His eyes twinkled with mischief.

"Attempted murder, terrorism, smuggling, money laundering and counterfeiting, that's all." Sarah laughed as she signed out of her computer.

"What about your cousin?"

"According to Miss Marple here, that case is still open."

Bernard raised his eyebrows at Rachel. "Well, you'd better get on with it. Your husband's being discharged tomorrow. Graham's just told me his kidneys are back to normal."

"Oh, that's wonderful news." Rachel hugged Bernard.

"That's if there are no more attempts on his life overnight. Speaking of which, I'm gutted I missed the Brillo escapade. I would have so loved to have seen her bound and gagged in the laundry cupboard."

They laughed loudly, but even that didn't wake Carlos. Rachel went over to his bed and kissed him on the forehead.

"Sarah and I are going for a drink," she told Bernard. "Do you mind if I come back and stay the night again? You know how much I love this infirmary. Not."

"We aim to please. Of course you can. You can use the bed next to him. You should get some sleep, you know." He whispered, "Sparky's on call tonight, so Gwen's taking the nurse on-call for Brigitte because Sparky believes Brigitte locked her in the cupboard."

"Sparky?" asked Sarah with raised eyebrows.

"It's my new nickname for Brillo. Her hair looks like she's put her finger in an electric socket, so Sparky suits her. It was either that or Frankenstein's monster, but I didn't want to insult the monster."

Rachel laughed again and Sarah thumped him playfully on the arm.

"Bernard Guinto, you're—"

"Amazing, I know. Now you two get out of here while I keep a close eye on our patient and hope no-one else is admitted. Although Sparky could become radioactive, in which case the laundry room would be the best place for her. Why didn't I think of locking her in there?"

Sarah wagged her finger at the incorrigible male nurse and Rachel took her arm.

"Time for that drink."

# Chapter 29

Rachel ran around the track on deck sixteen, enjoying the bright morning sun. Today was a sea day and Carlos was being discharged at lunchtime. He had slept so soundly that Bernard persuaded her to return to her own suite to get some quality sleep.

She felt refreshed and optimistic about the rest of her honeymoon. The only issue was that she hadn't worked out for certain who had killed Keith. Waverley seemed keen to accept the murder/suicide version that Jean had come up with.

She paused at the ship's inner rail and took in the view of the Lido Deck, where she had seen Carlos chatting with Helena four days before. The sun beat down on her back and light flickered off the still swimming pool. It wouldn't be long before it was packed with swimmers enjoying the day at sea. Some early arrivals were already commandeering sunbeds, choosing the best spot to spend their day.

As she glanced around at the scene, she saw a female crew member checking fire extinguishers and other safety equipment around the edge of the pool area. Then it hit her.

*Rachel Prince, how could you have been so stupid?* she scolded herself. *It's been staring you in the face all along.*

Racing back downstairs to her suite for a shower and a change, she then called Waverley, breathless with excitement.

"I know who killed Keith Bird," she said.

"Yes, Luke Connelly. Have you been drinking, Rachel? You sound strange."

"No. It's this phone, it's been playing up for days. Muffles every conversation I have with Sarah. No, Jack, it wasn't Luke. Can you meet me in the buffet? I'm just going up for breakfast."

She almost heard Waverley's brain whirring.

"If you insist. I hope you've got good reason to accuse someone else of murder. Just when I was hoping for a few days dealing with petty crime and crew fights."

He put the phone down.

Rachel ran back upstairs to the buffet and grabbed herself some fruit and cereal for breakfast. She found a table and asked a waiter for a pot of strong coffee. The lack of sleep was catching up with her, and she wanted to be in control of her faculties.

Waverley sat down and ordered a pot of tea.

"Well?"

"I've been an idiot. I should have guessed yesterday after the death of Luke Connelly. It was all too neat, you see? Then we were sidetracked thinking it might be Farmer who killed Keith, but when I saw the fire extinguisher by the pool this morning, I remembered something."

Waverley sighed heavily, clearly impatient with her ramblings and wanting her to get to the point. She smiled, remembering how Marjorie always liked to take her time over things; she would have enjoyed listening to the background. More so, she would have revelled in the security chief's impatience.

"Are you going to tell me what this is all about sometime today?" The chief's patience was running thin.

Rachel's mobile pinged and she saw she had a message from Sarah.

"Hang on a minute, I'll just check this in case something's happened to Carlos."

She felt the blood drain from her face as she listened to the message. Then she jumped up from the chair.

"We need to go. Now."

Rachel had to give Waverley credit that he trusted her enough to leap up from his seat and follow her.

"Where are we going?" He sounded breathless, trying to keep up as she ran down eight flights of stairs to deck eight. She raced along the corridor.

"Jean Sutton's room."

As they got there, the stateroom steward was coming out.

"Where's Miss Sutton?" Rachel asked.

"She went for breakfast, ma'am." Seeing Waverley, the man looked frightened. "Is something wrong, sir?"

"Have you seen Nurse Bradshaw?" Rachel snapped.

"Yes. She was with Miss Sutton, and then she left."

"With Miss Sutton?"

"No, ma'am, a few minutes before."

"Which way?"

"That way, ma'am. I think she went to see Mr Fairchild."

Rachel moved on to Duncan's stateroom.

"Quick, open the door," she commanded.

The steward opened the door to Duncan's room and Rachel burst through, leaving it to shut on the chief of security. Duncan came out of the shower with a towel round his waist.

"Where is she?"

"Where's who?" a bemused Duncan asked.

To Rachel's relief, Sarah appeared from under the bed. Rachel's eyes rolled.

"You're going to have to stop hiding under passengers' beds."

Sarah grinned sheepishly.

"I heard him come back in and was going to escape while he was in the shower. Rachel, it's him. He killed Keith."

"I know. I worked that out this morning."

Duncan followed the exchange between the two women with his mouth open.

"Will someone tell me what's going on here, because I don't know what you're talking about," he shouted. "I insist you leave this room now or I'll call security."

Waverley coughed from behind him. "You called?"

"These women have burst into my room and made all sorts of crazy allegations. You need to ask them to leave."

Waverley walked through into the lounge area and sat down in a comfy chair.

"What allegations?"

"I recognised the legs," said Sarah. "He has a birthmark on the back of the right calf. I remember seeing it on the day I hid under Farmer's bed."

Waverley coughed. "Under where?"

"Never mind that now, Chief," said Rachel. "Duncan killed Keith and tried to frame Jean for the murder, and when that didn't work, he killed Luke to frame him instead. As Luke couldn't defend himself, everyone believed Duncan's story. Duncan sowed the seeds, and Jean jumped to the conclusion that Luke was suicidal because he'd killed Keith."

"You haven't got one shred of evidence to back up what you're saying. It's preposterous. Keith was my friend; he could have been more than that if he hadn't been straight. I had no reason to kill him."

"Oh, but you did," said Rachel. "You were having an affair with Andrew Farmer. Did Keith threaten to expose him, or did you find out he was going to from the loose-tongued Jean?"

"Jean confirmed it was Farmer that Duncan had been seeing," said Sarah, "although she thought it was over when she saw Farmer with another man."

"What other man?" yelled Duncan.

"Oh, you thought your relationship was exclusive, did you?" chided Rachel. "Farmer has a string of toy boys like you ready to do his bidding."

"I don't believe you."

"Perhaps we could get back to the murder of Keith Bird and Luke Connelly," said Waverley. "I have little interest in the sordid love triangles of Mr Farmer or Mr Fairchild."

"Duncan was in love with Farmer. When Farmer heard about the cruise, they arranged to meet up and continue their affair. Keith had found the papers implicating Farmer in corruption that we know about and, more worrying for Keith, Farmer's links to the Mafia. Keith was frightened, but planned to expose Farmer somehow. If he hadn't managed to speak to me, he probably planned to leave the papers somewhere they could be found and acted upon.

"Max said Keith was spooked the night he was in the Cigar Lounge. I believe he saw Farmer and was afraid the man had discovered he'd picked up his briefcase when he left it in the salon. Which he had, of course. Duncan argued with Keith on the first night of the cruise and killed him.

"You see, Duncan, you made a mistake. You told us on the coach that Keith had been hit over the back of the head with a fire extinguisher – a fact only the killer would know. I knew something bothered me about your story, but didn't put it together until today. You also visited Farmer on the third day while Sarah here was, erm," Rachel looked at Waverley, "checking his room."

Waverley rolled his eyes, but said nothing.

"I bet Farmer was furious when you told him you'd planted his documents in Jean's room."

Duncan deflated. "He was. I didn't know the files were in there. When he told me, I tried to get them back, but they were gone."

"Why did you try to frame Miss Sutton?" asked Waverley, finding his tongue.

"She's got a big gob, that's why. Her gossip caused me and Keith to argue. You're right, Keith was going to expose Andrew. I pleaded with him not to that night. He was drunk; he laughed in my face. I didn't mean to kill him. I just grabbed the first thing to hand and hit him. He fell. I knew he was dead, so I shoved him in the pool to make it look like an accident."

"Why did you take Keith's room key?" asked Sarah.

Duncan shrugged. "I'd been in his room earlier and seen him put a load of cash in a drawer. I figured he wouldn't need his money anymore, so I went to his room and took it. I found the folder in a drawer, thinking it was his dodgy deal accounts." Duncan looked up. "He was no saint. He fiddled the books, took huge cash advances and wasn't averse to a bit of blackmail on the side. I'd checked the folder before. How was I to know he'd switched papers or folder? I really didn't mean to kill him. We were close, or could have been."

"Maybe not, but you did mean to kill Luke Connelly when your first plan didn't work." Rachel glared at the man.

"Get dressed, Mr Fairchild. I have just about enough room in the ship's brig for you," said Waverley. "Thank you, Rachel, and to you, Sarah, but I don't want to hear anything else about you hiding under passenger beds ever again. Do you understand?"

"Yes, sir," said Sarah.

"Neither do I, Sarah Bradshaw," said Rachel, laughing.

# Chapter 30

When Rachel walked into the infirmary, the medical team were all there, minus Brillo Sin, and she entered to a huge round of applause. Helena sat with Carlos, and they too clapped as she entered.

"What's this all about?" she asked.

Bernard was the first to speak.

"The magnificent and beautiful Rachel Prince… sorry, Rachel Jacobi-Prince does it again. Now she's set to ride into the sunset with the love of her life and live happily ever after."

Rachel blushed.

"He watches far too many old Westerns," said Gwen, grinning. "Congratulations, Rachel, you've managed to save lives and catch killers once again."

"It wasn't all me. This time I have to share the praise with Sarah, my husband and Helena."

Sarah beamed at the compliment.

"Without their help, I'd be minus a husband, and we wouldn't have found Helena in time, so we'll share this one. Where's the new doctor?"

"Packing," said Dr Bentley. "It appears she doesn't enjoy cruise ship life and is disembarking in Ajaccio tomorrow. She'll make her own way home."

"Doesn't that leave you short of a doctor?"

"It does, but the crew are being remarkably understanding and have promised me they won't be ill until we find a replacement."

"Yeah, right," laughed Gwen.

"And we have promised to cover the extra shifts. Anything to see the back of that woman," said Brigitte. "It was her or me."

"I'm glad you didn't threaten me with that one," said Gwen, "or you might have found yourself out of a job."

Bernard nudged his French friend.

"Don't worry, she's only kidding. I'm still gutted nobody recorded the doctor in the cupboard episode. I could have posted it online. It would have gone viral."

"Anyway, Rachel, as you can see, your husband is fit and well again, and if you both promise to stay out of trouble for the rest of the cruise, you can continue your honeymoon with our blessing."

Rachel caught the longing in Carlos's eye.

"I think I know just the thing to keep him out of mischief."

THE END

# Author's Note

Thank you for reading *Honeymoon Cruise Murder*, the seventh book in my Rachel Prince Mystery series. If you have enjoyed it, please leave an honest review on Amazon and/or any other platform you may use. I love receiving feedback from readers and can assure you that I read every review.

## Keep in touch:

Sign up for my no-spam newsletter at:
https://www.dawnbrookespublishing.com

Follow me on Facebook:
https://www.facebook.com/dawnbrookespublishing/

Follow me on Twitter:
@dawnbrookes1

Follow me on Pinterest:
https://www.pinterest.co.uk/dawnbrookespublishing

# Books by Dawn Brookes

## Rachel Prince Mysteries

A Cruise to Murder

Deadly Cruise

Killer Cruise

Dying to Cruise

A Christmas Cruise Murder

Murderous Cruise Habit

Honeymoon Cruise Murder

## Memoirs

Hurry up Nurse: memoirs of nurse training in the
1970s

Hurry up Nurse 2: London calling

Hurry up Nurse 3: More adventures in the life of a
student nurse

## Coming Soon 2020

Book 8 in the *Rachel Prince Mystery* series

A Murder Mystery Cruise

Look out for a Carlos Jacobi crime novel in 2020

Body in the Woods

## Picture Books for Children

Ava & Oliver's Bonfire Night Adventure
Ava & Oliver's Christmas Nativity Adventure
Danny the Caterpillar
Gerry the One-Eared Cat
Suki Seal and the Plastic Ring

# Acknowledgements

Thank you to my editor Alison Jack, as always, for her kind comments about the book and for suggestions, corrections and amendments that make it a more polished read. Thanks to Alex Davis for the final proofread, corrections and suggestions.

Thanks to my beta readers for comments and suggestions, and for their time given to reading the early drafts.

Thanks to my immediate circle of friends who are so patient with me when I'm absorbed in my fictional world and for your continued support in all my endeavours.

I have to say thank you to my cruise-loving friends for joining me on some of the most precious experiences of my life, and to the cruise lines for making every holiday a special one.

# About the Author

Dawn Brookes is author of the *Rachel Prince Mystery* series, combining a unique blend of murder, cruising and medicine with a touch of romance.

Dawn has a 39-year nursing pedigree and takes regular cruise holidays, which she says are for research purposes! She brings these passions together with a Christian background and a love of clean crime to her writing.

The surname of her protagonist is in honour of her childhood dog, Prince, who used to put his head on her knee while she lost herself in books.

Bestselling author of *Hurry up Nurse: memoirs of nurse training in the 1970s* and *Hurry up Nurse 2: London calling*, Dawn worked as a hospital nurse, midwife, district nurse and community matron across her career. Before turning her hand to writing for a living, she had multiple articles published in professional journals and coedited a nursing textbook.

She grew up in Leicester, later moved to London and Berkshire, but now lives in Derbyshire. Dawn holds a

Bachelor's degree with Honours and a Master's degree in education. Writing across genres, she also writes for children. Dawn has a passion for nature and loves animals, especially dogs. Animals will continue to feature in her children's books, as she believes caring for animals and nature helps children to become kinder human beings.